MICK JAWOR

A DEADLY MEMORY

What happened to
Joe's beautiful wife
- and can he face
the truth about
their marriage?

MICK JAWOR

A DEADLY
MEMORY

What happened to
Joe's beautiful wife
- and can he face
the truth about
their marriage?

MEREO
Cirencester

Mereo Books

1A The Wool Market Dyer Street Cirencester Gloucestershire GL7 2PR
An imprint of Memoirs Publishing www.mereobooks.com

A Deadly Memory: 978-1-86151-756-2

First published in Great Britain in 2017
by Mereo Books, an imprint of Memoirs Publishing

The address for Memoirs Publishing Group Limited can be found at www.memoirspublishing.com

The Memoirs Publishing Group Ltd Reg. No. 7834348

The Memoirs Publishing Group supports both The Forest Stewardship Council® (FSC®) and the PEFC® leading international forest-certification organisations. Our books carrying both the FSC label and the PEFC® and are printed on FSC®-certified paper. FSC® is the only forest-certification scheme supported by the leading environmental organisations including Greenpeace. Our paper procurement policy can be found at www.memoirspublishing.com/environment

Typeset in 11/17pt Century Schoolbook
by Wiltshire Associates Publisher Services Ltd. Printed and bound in Great Britain by Marston Book Services Ltd, Oxfordshire

This book is dedicated to all the families who have had to endure the insanity of alcohol and have been brave enough see it through to recovery and come out the other side intact.

Special thanks to all the people who did their little bit in getting this here, especially Russell and Car – they know. And all the people who have shaped this book, they know who they are as well.

Quoted song lyrics - acknowledgments

Rollon - Kid Rock
No Surrender - Bruce Springsteen
Do You Feel - Peter Frampton
Against the Wind - Bob Seeger
Red - Daniel Merriweather
Strong Persuader - Robert Cray
While I can dream - Elvis Presley @IMGEM U.S.LLC

PROLOGUE

Hi. My name is Joe Donaldson, and I'm sixty-five years old. Well, not quite – I'll be sixty-five next week, so my two boys are coming over for my birthday and also for my retirement, although I am not officially retiring, because after spending forty-five years in the corporate world I have spent the last three working for a local hardware store, just for something to do, and I was hoping to continue there for at least another couple of years.

Luke and Taylor are the most important things in my life. Luke, the elder, is at university studying Sports Science, whatever that is, and Taylor, 13 months younger, is also at university, doing Drama. I'm not really sure what that is either, must be a generation thing, it was chemistry, biology, maths or physics that was most popular at university in my time, that's what you needed to get a good job. But at 21 and 20, they are smart, hardworking, honest boys, boys you would be proud of, boys whose parents have loved, nurtured and shaped them into grown-ups. Well I tried my best, especially after losing their mother over 10 years ago. I cut down my hours and devoted my time to be there for them. I didn't miss a football match or a Christmas play, and in their late teenage years I was the taxi driver, bank and dogsbody that all dads turn into. That doesn't mean we didn't disagree or argue, we did, over homework initially, then suitable girlfriends and how late they would get in, if at all, normal family stuff. All that changed when they took residence at their respective universities, when I finally had to let go.

So they're coming over on Saturday and we are all going out for lunch. I have two things to tell them, one a recent bit of news, one an old bit of news. They don't know yet that I have been diagnosed with cancer and now have between three and six months to live, that's the recent news. There goes my three-year working plan.

The old news, believe it or not, that's the harder one to talk about. When the kids were small they used to ask questions: 'Dad, have you ever been in a police car?' 'Dad, did you ever steal anything?' The usual questions, I guess. Anyway what you tell your children when they are young is a difficult choice. Do they want to know that their dad still remembers stealing from the local sweet shop, getting caught drink driving, taking drugs at parties, getting married and divorced, becoming an alcoholic?

Luckily I turned my life around before the two of them arrived. I don't think they need to know everything. Life is a rollercoaster, and when you're young it seems the highs and lows are a lot higher and lower than when you get older, or is it that the level of steepness is the same but the ability to deal with it becomes somewhat greater? I guess everyone tells their children different things at different ages. Responding to a ten-year-old's question 'ever been in a police car, Dad?' with the answer 'no' but providing words of wisdom to a fifteen-year-old under the guise of 'don't do what I did' with the answer 'yes' could be deemed hypocritical. There is no correct answer. However, when you know that your rollercoaster is coming to the end of the line you have a different perspective; when you look back on life what do you want, or not want, your children to know, or should they know everything?

So over lunch I'm going to tell them the recent news first, and then I think I'll tell them the old news, but I'm still not sure. They remember a lot about their lives, particularly the immediate years before and after their mother died, but only now, if I tell them the truth, will they realise and understand the causes and effects that shaped our lives.

I don't know, you decide.

'Roll on, roll on, rollercoaster, you are one day older and one day closer.'

CONTENTS

People can be cruel, and they will be. People can hurt
you, break your heart, and they will.
But only YOU can let them KEEP hurting you.

CHAPTER 1

THE END

The boys jumped into the car; it was pickup time from school. They settled down and demanded that the CD player was cranked up; disc 5 track 11 – Bruce Springsteen's *No Surrender*. As the harmonica echoed around the car the boys ate their chocolate bars and began singing – '*busted out of school, had no time for the fools, we learnt more from three minute records than we ever learnt from school...*' They sang as they did at church on a Saturday night, a bit too much gusto and not enough melody, but they knew the words.

A little sadness reached out and touched me. It hadn't been the best week at home, in fact it hadn't been a good year and it was only February. The year before hadn't been good either.

It's only a four-minute drive home, but there was just enough time for the track to finish as we pulled up on the driveway. You could see the Thames flowing serenely by at the back of the house as the swans were settling in their groups for the late afternoon siesta before the walkers arrived, feeding them bread and other leftovers.

Their mum's car was parked in the driveway, and the boys shouted expectantly, 'Mummy's home!' Not that this was unusual, but more infrequent than frequent. Through the patio windows they could see Mummy lying on the settee. As we disembarked I picked up the school bags and lunch boxes and strode towards the door as the kids waited for me, banging loudly as sometimes Kate comes and opens the door, and sometimes she doesn't.

I unlocked the door and the kids rushed through, kicked off their shoes, shook off their coats and shouted 'hello!' as they ran upstairs to play the Xbox. With bags and boxes in one hand I collected the shoes, hung up the coats, walked into the lounge without taking my coat off, then I looked around.

I said 'Hello, how's things?' There was no response,

so I walked past her into the kitchen carrying my wares.

The kitchen looked like a bomb had hit it. Breakfast plates and food cartoons had not been put away, the dishwasher was still full from last night, the takeaway cartons were lying on the floor; the recycling hadn't been taken out and next to the sink were three empty bottles of Pinot Grigio. I started tidying, working quietly as the kids banged around upstairs; I didn't want to wake her.

After the kitchen was reassembled, I picked up the wine bottles to take to the bins outside. Walking past Kate lying on the settee, I didn't hear her stir; normally there would be a snore, a snort or a deep sigh, as she was a noisy sleeper. Quite often if she was disturbed she would turn over, swearing loudly or just talking gibberish, a disturbed sleep pattern that was exasperated by alcohol. I just ignored it when it happened.

I was angry. We had spent a lot of money and effort trying to address the alcohol consumption and the subsequent behaviour that followed. Outside, instead of putting the wine bottles down gently, I smashed them into the recycling bin. Glass flew everywhere, and suddenly I felt calmer.

Deep breath. It's Monday night, the bin men arrive on Tuesday mornings, no one would see the shattered bottles reduced to a small mountain of glass shards.

Although we had been seeing a therapist nearly every two weeks for nine months, there had been very little acceptance from Kate that she had a problem. Don't get me wrong, she knew she had a problem and understood how it affected our family, but why should she change? There was always a reason, no matter how large or small, that would kick start a binge.

Last night's argument with me and the kids hadn't helped, nor had the three bottles of wine consumed yesterday, and it was so trivial. The boys had wanted to watch a DVD but couldn't decide which one. They ended up agreeing on *How To Train Your Dragon,* but as they were loading the disc she decided she didn't want to watch it and turned the television off. We sat for 30 minutes staring at a blank screen.

I have learnt when to keep quiet as I didn't want a scene, especially in front of the boys. With all that has been going on they too have learned not to cause a fuss, as the fallout is often unpredictable. I had gone into the kitchen and suggested we put the television on and watch something funny, thinking this could defuse the tension, but she jumped off the settee and punched me in the stomach. It didn't hurt, but the effect on the children was visible. She stormed off out the back door for a cigarette; I took the kids to another room to watch television and closed the door. She finished her cigarette and went back into the house, swearing at me as she walked past the closed door.

The boys and I watched TV, huddled together. We had supper, played cards quietly and eventually I took them to bed. We said goodnight to Mummy as we walked past the closed door; I always made them say goodnight, even if it was a one-way salutation.

She must have come to bed about 2am. I lay there pretending to be asleep as she got into bed, pulled the covers off me and curled into a ball. I gave it 10 minutes, then went downstairs and turned all the lights and the gas fire off, tidied up, then crept back to bed; I don't think she remembered anything when I got up the next morning. She stayed in bed while I got the kids up, washed, dressed and fed them ready for school. We shouted our goodbyes and left her.

I put out the recycling bin, with glass rattling around inside it. It's been a busy day so far. I went for an interview in London, then headed straight from the railway station to pick the kids up from school. My guess is that she just woke up this morning after I had taken the boys to school, came downstairs and started drinking again; looking at her asleep on the settee, I wonder where all the good times went.

I lean in closer, because she hasn't moved since we got home, and maybe 10 minutes have passed. Then I see that her eyes are open and just visible over the cushions facing the wall.

I call out quietly to try and stir her. I turn her over, but there's no movement. I listen for a breath, but there's nothing; I reach out and brush her arm with my hand, and realise her skin is cold to the touch.

My heart beats faster, but everything seems to be going slower. I can hear the kids arguing, and the television is still on, but I can't hear it.

I pull back and stand very still for a few seconds; no panic, no wailing and no tears. I reach for my mobile phone in my jacket pocket and calmly dial the emergency services. My mind's wandering. When was the last time I called 999? Have I ever called them? I feel that somewhere deep inside I was already prepared for this moment, I just didn't know it would be today.

'You say you're tired, want to close your eyes and follow your dream down; no retreat baby, no surrender.'

What is normal within a household? What is a normal relationship, what is too much to drink? What is depression? I learnt as an adult that I preferred to keep an even keel; life is too short to go large on the happy times and pay for it large in the low times. Since having children I have believed in a calm house that would suit the children, that would help them, enable them to grow and mature in a safe and stable environment. Children do not need parents screaming and shouting at each other. I have seen how my boys react. They should not be scared in their own home, or worried about what is going to happen next. We even had a stencil on one of the walls: "May this home be blessed with the laughter of children, the warmth of a close family, hope for the future and fond memories of the past". My memories have been difficult to describe as fond, as the dark memories overshadow the good ones and it seems a long time since I first noticed that the close family and the blessed house were not so close and not so blessed, certainly not as I had imagined them to be.

CHAPTER 2

THE START

When did it all start?

I guess Kate and I were both social people, with professional jobs, working hard and playing hard after the five o'clock bell. We met in a pub and spent two or three years being friends whilst seeing other people. I went away for a couple of weeks and came back to find her wanting to be my girlfriend, and she moved in the next week. After a few years of living together we talked about having kids, and lo and behold within two years we had two boys. I understand that children born twelve months apart are called Irish twins; ours were born thirteen months apart.

So in a short period of time we went from going out nearly every night to being controlled by two boys. She gave up work and I went from job to job, spending as much time as I could at home. I found it difficult to keep my career going when I had so many demands at home, many times she offered to help with the kids after school schedule, many times she failed to deliver. Her biggest challenge was drifting between boredom and chaos, night and day.

The first years were spent nappy changing, feeding, playing with toys and generally being proud of our two little ones. There were times when it became too much and I would come home to find she had been on the wine throughout the day, so I had to take over and bring the place back together. Once I was on a teleconference with my boss when she came into the makeshift office dragging the two boys behind her - they must have been about three and four at the time – and dumped them on me, both crying. She just walked out of the door, jumped into the car and sped off. The kids and I slept on the floor downstairs waiting for her to come home, the three of us wrapped in a ball of arms and legs, but she didn't return until the morning. No explanation, no recrimination; she was just full, had had enough.

There were other times when the wine became her crutch, and reaching for the bottle in times of stress became reaching for the bottle whenever she could. In her more lucid moments she would tell me that she didn't remember a lot of the time we spent with the kids and wished she did.

Weekends were spent with me taking the boys out, museums, play areas, anywhere we could to keep out of the house. The three of us were on an adventure, and I think I deliberately tried to fill the Saturdays and Sundays with as much fun and laughter as I could. Football golf, tennis – you name it, we did it, arriving home shattered, but all three of us had a story and a smile.

Luke and Taylor were soon at nursery. We also had baby sitters and cleaners throughout the early years, but she still found her life a major challenge. We talked about the issues and what I could do for her. We talked about depression and who could help her. I was out of my depth. The doctor prescribed pills and more pills, but we never saw any improvement.

We scrabbled through the first years and the kids started to grow up and go to school, I thought this would provide some respite, but the problem changed from having too much to do to not having enough. The house would be cleaned and re-cleaned; she started working in a career that gave her an out. Most weekends she would be up early and back late and I would have the boys.

For her, the booze was always there, and during the week the temptation got to her. With nothing to do and no close friends to spend time with, the pub at lunchtime seemed a good place to spend a couple of hours; then a bottle of wine at home, so by the time I got back from work I was walking into a war zone. She had fallen out with the kids and herself and I had to pick up the pieces. It often turned into arguments over nothing. An argument is normal when two people disagree; this was more of a one-way demolition of me. If I was five minutes late home I would be in for it, and if I was five minutes early I would be in for it.

Things went from bad to worse, and then she started going out with people I never met – sounds like such an obvious issue, looking back. The reasoning was that I had been out working all day, ergo it was my turn to look after the kids so she could go out, and what was wrong with her going to the pub for a couple of hours?

Sometimes I would ask her not to go and say maybe we could do something with the kids. Sometimes the kids would ask her not to go, but she read that as me setting the kids against her and went anyway. It got so bad that one of the boys would stand at the door to bar her way, but she would physically push past him and slam the door behind her. She wouldn't listen to me trying to reason with her.

As the next month rolled to a close we lurched from one situation to another. I even began to wonder if she really was working on a Saturday night or if she was out somewhere else. In between the situations there were some moments of respite, a day off the wine, a couple of days at Centre Parcs. There were some good times, and we even talked about extending the family to three.

During the next couple of months, the pattern continued, with the odd night of not coming back till late, more frequent lunchtime sessions and no comfort at home. I found her one night outside the front door sitting on the step; she had fallen over on the way home and couldn't find her key. I opened the door and she fell inside, wanting to know why was I still up, and was I checking up on her? Many a time she would come in and sleep on the settee downstairs. The mornings after were worse, as she would reach for the bottle early to cure the hangover. I would call her in the day from work to find that the kids had not gone to school and they were all going to the pub for lunch, as she wanted to spend some quality time with them.

The first big step change happened a few months later, on a cold and miserable November evening. She came home at about 2am and was totally blitzed. I was in bed, and when she fell into the bedroom I asked if she had been out with her boyfriend. She flipped and accused me of ruining her life. I was angry but controlled and went downstairs; I crept into bed later without waking her. What do you say? I had no proof, just suspicions. Deep down I really knew something was broken and I didn't know how to fix it.

I got up early the next morning and got the boys dressed, washed and fed all within an hour. I took a lot less time to get myself ready, washed, suit on, PC in my rucksack. I dropped them at school; she had stayed in bed.

I got an emergency call from her at work in the early afternoon of the same day - could I come home as soon as possible? I could tell she had been drinking. This wasn't in itself unusual but there was a certain edge in her voice, something was wrong, very wrong. I asked if I should pick up the kids, but she had arranged for one of the mums to have both for a couple of hours. The hairs on my neck and arms bristled. I excused myself from work and made my way home. What's up this time? What could be so monumental that I had to come home straight away? I knew the boys were ok.

As I turned into the drive and made my way to the front door, I was still wondering. I did not want to enter the house, but at the same time I knew I had to.

I unlocked the door and went through the hall to the front room. The TV was on, so I assumed that was where she would be. I sat down on the settee next to her. the front room was strewn with bottles of wine, empty, obviously. She asked if I wanted a drink; I politely refused and asked 'what's up?'

She looked a mess. She had been crying, her mascara had run, the long, flowing blonde locks, naturally curly, which turned every man's head, were in tatters, and clumps of hair were visible on her shoulders and T-shirt. It appeared that she had been trying to pull it out with her fingers. She tried to talk, to say hello, but then stopped, inhaled deeply, leaned forward and looked me in the eye.

'I slept with someone else last night. I don't know why but I did, that's it, I said it.'

Some things in this world you don't want to hear, and that's one of them.

CHAPTER 3

HAPPY XMAS

How do you deal with this? I guess everyone is different. Did I hit her? Did I shout and scream? Did I kick her out? Did I kill her in a fit of rage?

To be honest I can't remember what I did, but I know I did not do any of the above. Deep down I knew something was up. We had gone into the pub a few times and she had befriended a few guys that hung around together. It was obvious that some of the guys fancied her and I had mentioned it several times, but the retort was, 'they are just friends, can't guys just be friends?' Then there were the texts and hiding her phone, explaining that an old friend had got back in touch with her.

We talked for a while, she apologised profusely, said it was a mistake, she had taken cocaine and couldn't remember anything, said it would never happen again. I asked if I knew him and she said no, but I knew it was one of the guys from the pub. By sheer coincidence the local paper had done a feature on the pub and taken some photos of the regulars; the main mug shot was of a guy called Nick. She had tried to hide the paper from me but eventually she showed me.

So now I knew who she had slept with, when and what had happened. Was that meant to make me feel better? She couldn't tell me why; I asked but got no reply. She explained that she didn't want us to split up and if I could forgive her then she would stop drinking or going to the pub. I had to think. Everything was caving in on me, yet it felt like it was her who was the victim. Why did I feel like this?

I went and picked the kids up and brought them home, and nothing was said. We acted as if nothing had happened. Everything was normal on the surface, but deep down I was boiling. Somehow, maybe irrationally, I thought she had been very brave in telling me what she had done, but a bigger part was telling me I wished she hadn't.

When you reach into the bottom of the well and it is empty, you think nothing else can go wrong, but life has a cruel way of sending you one step further.

The next day and the few days following she didn't go to the pub. I tried to remain calm and we avoided any possible conversation around the boys. I think they would have been too young to pick up on the turmoil but as I found out later, children can be very perceptive.

The next week we talked some more and I said I didn't want her to leave, mainly I guess because of the boys, but I also thought everyone should have a second chance and if we could get through this together then maybe it would make us stronger. She said she would never speak to the guy again and I accepted that.

She didn't go out for a while. Christmas was coming and we had to get the house ready and special for Luke and Taylor, buy and wrap all the toys and deck the house out, and we were generally very busy. The boys were getting more and more excited and we were settling down to a routine or pattern of life. The elephant was very much still in the room, but if we avoided it then maybe it would disappear.

A couple of weeks after the big step change I got another emergency call at work. She didn't normally call me - she might text but not call - so as I answered

I knew there was another problem coming. She explained that the police were at the house and could I tell her where the insurance certificates were for the car. I had bought her a new car when the kids were born and as it was still in my name the police were looking for me to verify that it was legally insured. I wanted to ask more, but was told she would tell me when I got home.

I left work, thinking it couldn't be any worse than the last time she called, and rushed home to another disaster. Sure enough she was sitting on the settee, empty bottle by her side, looking just as distraught as the week before.

She started to explain. After drinking all morning she had decided to go and see Nick and tell him that she wasn't talking to him ever again; I guess he had been texting asking for further affection. She drove the half mile to his house and crashed into a parked car, and without stopping she had driven back home. A witness had seen this and reported the number plate, which was in my name, so the police had arrived at the house looking for me. I understand that she told the police the whole story, pleaded guilty to everything and spent the next 20 minutes crying. As the insurance certificates were all in check they unbelievably gave her a warning and let her off.

As you might expect, I was furious. Not only was the car badly damaged but what in hell did she think she was doing? Her answer was that she was closing this chapter and wanted to make sure he wouldn't contact her again, and she started crying.

The next day she spent in bed, and the day after. It was just two weeks before Christmas and I could see she wasn't well, mentally or physically. Then, just to top off the end of our *annus horribilis*, she was sick in the morning.

You guessed it. There are some things said in this world that you don't want to hear and it seemed like this was my year for hearing them all.

I was pottering around in the kitchen, after taking the boys for the last day at school before the term ended. They were both on dress-down day and had picked their favourite football kit to wear. Only the three of us had eaten breakfast together; apart from an hour at the shops the day before we hadn't really seen her, as she had spent the past 48 hours in bed. I had just finished loading the dishwasher when something caught my eye. I looked around to see her leaning on the door jamb with what looked like a toothbrush in her hand.

'I'm pregnant and it's not yours,' she said.

No great opening, no apology, no feelings, nothing, just a factual statement that I was supposed to accept as a fact and deal with. She would get rid of it as soon as medically possible, she said. That was nice to know!

Now should I hit her, or should I just kill her as she stood there, wipe that supercilious look of her face for once and for all? My life was totally out of control. I thought I had just made the ultimate sacrifice in forgiving her; now just as I picked myself up she had knocked me back down again. Did I love her or hate her?

How do you deal with this? Polite conversation over breakfast – 'Don't worry honey, I'll clean up your vomit', 'your tits are looking bigger', 'by the way, how is the little bastard?' What can you say when the person sleeping next to you has someone else's baby growing inside them? Do you just ignore it, block it out, pretend it's a dream? Effectively it's a nightmare, of immense proportions. It could not have happened to us. With Christmas on the horizon we took the easy route; we didn't talk about it.

Then Christmas Day arrived. The kids were playing on the Santa-delivered Wii whilst we lounged around the house, and a few glasses of champagne later we found ourselves alone in the other room. The argument started with the kids and escalated into an issue that I was to blame for; I suggested she should calm down when everything kicked off. She came at me and threw a couple of punches, and I slapped her around the head and sent her back into the chair, followed by a shout of 'Take your bastard kid out of this house!' That was the first and only time I have ever hit a woman. I was so ashamed of myself. I know I am not a violent man, never have been. What had she made me do? If I could hit her, could I kill her?

She immediately went in and told the kids that Dad had just hit her and we were splitting up. Dad was leaving the house today. The boys understandably were upset - they didn't understand the complexities of our relationship, how could they? I didn't either. They sat huddled in the corner, arms wrapped around each other, sobbing; that vision was heart-breaking to me, they looked so afraid, had I done that? Happy Fucking Christmas!

I apologised and we all calmed down, but that was a tough couple of days. I know what I had done was not acceptable, but I believed there was a significant degree of provocation. She was seeing herself as a victim, it was all about her, there was nothing on how I felt, I had no one to confide in, no one to console me. I tried my best to help her.

As expected, I paid for the abortion, which couldn't be done until mid-January, and paid for the car to be fixed. Then we spent our time treading carefully around each other for the next few months. The elephant was still in the room.

CHAPTER 4

THE INTERVIEW

The police asked for an interview with me two days after her body had been taken away; they wanted to talk to the children as well, and I gave permission as long as they had someone with them. Mother-in-law kindly volunteered and we all agreed that it would be best if this was conducted around the house. The boys were interviewed first and then my mother-in law took them out to the cinema.

Detective Inspector James Cooper, a tall, gaunt

man about the same age as me, obviously ex-military, and a female officer called Leann something – I missed her

surname – came into the kitchen and sat down. I offered tea, and they gratefully accepted. I tidied up the kitchen table, where I had left some notes and papers that I had been preparing that morning.

I asked if the interviews with the children had been productive, to which they responded that they would like to talk to me before they commented on anything. James, as he asked me to call him, explained that there would be a medical examination to find out the cause of death, but this might take a while and meantime they would like to go through a few items with me. I shrugged flippantly and mentioned something like 'I know the cause of death, it's been coming'. Leann already had her notebook out and wrote quickly.

In anticipation of the first question I suggested that I should start talking and hopefully most of the questions would be answered, and if there was anything else they could interrupt. I figured that if I volunteered as much as I knew, I would come across as though I had nothing to hide.

So I began. I brushed over how we had met and the first couple of years, before children, painting a picture of a happy couple, holidaying in the Maldives, cruises around the Med and moving into a small flat near the river. I explained my job and financial status, as I saw an eyebrow raised when I had mentioned the Maldives; I studied both faces as I talked.

I went on to describe the early years of moving into the current house, the times and dates of the children being born, 13 months apart. The stress and strain of parenthood, carefully mentioning how she had struggled with the boredom, late nights and constant attention required by two little nippers. There was very little interruption; just a few questions on my family and hers, brothers and sisters, addresses and if we had regular contact. I provided a small but detailed précis of how she and her older sister had fallen out and not talked for the past four years, although I kept in contact with her family so the boys could stay in touch with their cousins.

I was careful not to throw in the bad times and concentrated on telling the good stories and fond memories. I knew I was going to have to face the bad ones later.

I talked about schools, how we had opted for the local Catholic school as I was Catholic, although not religious, and how I had to take the kids to mass on Sundays to get them into the school, and it wasn't easy getting two boys to church on my own. I talked about holidays to Cyprus, Disneyland Paris and Spain; trips to Thorpe Park, Chessington, football on a Saturday morning, visiting Granddad and other random memories from that time. We had even bought a caravan so that we had an easy escape during the long summer school terms. I guess I said 'on my own' quite a lot, as several times I was interrupted with questions pertaining to where she was whilst I was doing all these activities with the kids. Beside the holidays, it was mainly me and the boys. She had part-time work from time to time or preferred staying at home, as she needed some 'me time.' At this point James was going to ask me for clarification, but Leann cut him off with a nod, as if to say, 'I know what you mean'.

To them our life must have seemed relatively idyllic, but I know at this point I was going to change the conversation; a lot of what I knew was private between me and Kate. The boys might have mentioned a few episodes. I don't think they remembered a particular Christmas Day, but I'm sure they would have mentioned some of the arguments. In addition I would bet that if they had canvassed the street or even popped into the pub some tongues would be wagging, so I steered into the dark times. I explained that drinking had become a crutch and how I had tried to control her alcohol consumption, though again it wasn't the drinking but the behaviour afterwards. I then went on to the episode where I had first heard the words that had made me think about killing her - not that I told them that. Poor Leann's pen and notebook were taking a hammering as I mentioned the other guy, the abortion, me hitting her on Christmas Day and the subsequent months of calm, contrition and reconciliation.

We decided somehow to take a break. I didn't realise we had been going for two and a half hours and the children would be back soon. I suggested that we continue the next day; I wanted to get out as much as possible and see where the straw would fall, what would be picked up and what would be discarded, the wheat and the chaff.

As they were leaving Leann turned over a new page in her notebook and asked for a list of people they could talk to. I think that was to verify my story, or parts of it, but also to see if they could find out anything I didn't know. I had already prepared a list, mostly of people I knew, her family, the landlady from the pub, the other guy (although I didn't know his phone number and address – stupid question that was), friends from school who had witnessed her picking the children up whilst pissed and driving.

The therapist's name was highlighted and stood out. I had mentioned her during the interview – Kaz. She had been Kate's therapist first before we had started seeing her together. During the interview this session had been the most interactive. I was asked why, who instigated it, what did we discuss, how often did we go, and the real question – why did we stop going?

I must have spent about half an hour on this and it definitely piqued the interest of Leann, who had been relatively passive up to this point. I explained that I had asked Kate to see someone after I had become so exasperated by her behaviour I didn't know what to do. She had chosen a therapist on the internet. She had gone on her own and initially she came back and told me what they had talked about. She was given a drinking diary to fill in, and did so meticulously. She even showed me what she had recorded. It was up to two or three bottles of wine a day, each bottle nine units, and we were up to 140 units per week, but Kate didn't see this as a problem. Kaz explained to me that it wasn't how much or what she drank, it was why. We started seeing Kaz together three months later, based on our relationship, communication, alcohol and intimacy; I didn't realise until we stopped going that these were my issues with the relationship and mine only. She didn't think there was anything amiss but just went along anyway.

Why did we stop going? She didn't want to go any more, she was fed up with being told that our relationship wasn't working because she wasn't putting any effort in and effectively it was all her fault. In a strange way, I could understand this; maybe I was flogging a dead horse. As I was talking Leann was studiously taken copious notes.

I had expected someone to ask for a list, so in my notes on the table I had also written down the name and phone number of my ex-wife, although I hadn't seen her for 15 years; we had had an amicable split and I was sure she had nothing bad to say about me (except of course about the affair that pushed us apart), and some email addresses of ex- girlfriends who kept in touch sporadically. When questioned about male friends I showed on the list a few guys from work that I kept in touch with, although they didn't really know me, a few guys from my football years whom I hadn't see for years, except at funerals and christenings, explaining that I didn't really go out much since I was looking after the kids. I added a tempter, that I was scared of leaving the kids with her sometimes.

Half way down the list was Kevin; name, address, and relationship to her, lover. When they asked who he was I said he was a neighbour who lived three doors down and I would tell them more about that story when we next met. I had already given enough in this session.

I also gave them the three letters, two from Nick

and one from Kevin, explaining that I had found them a couple of months before, hidden away at the back of a drawer. I had photocopied the letters and returned the originals, but when I had looked for the originals that morning they were not there. I had also labelled them as exhibit 1, a letter from Nick, exhibit 2, a letter from Kevin and exhibit 3, another from Nick.

We arranged to continue our session at 11am the next morning, same place, my house. This suited me as Kate's mother was staying and she could take the boys out. I didn't want them around in case it got difficult – not that it should, until the pathology results were released.

Leann also asked for a photograph of the two of us. There were none downstairs among the plethora of photos on the walls of her and the boys. I went to the office and returned with one of the few photographs we had, taken on a holiday several years before. I handed it over. Then I walked the officers to the door and shook their hands.

I wish I could have heard what was being said in the car as they drove off.

CHAPTER 5

EXHIBIT 1

So tell me why? The first time I saw you I wanted you, though I knew I had to wait till you were feeling vulnerable and lonely and needed a shoulder. You were pretty easy to lead down to my path. You listened when I told you there was another way, and you only live once, so why throw it away with your husband and kids?

In the bar when I got you alone I asked you to draw on a piece of paper, just doodle. Everyone draws a square or circle, sometime a cube. I had drawn all three on my piece of paper and you didn't know that I waited for you to show yours before I showed mine - hey ho, exactly the same. You were amazed that I could read your mind and understand how you felt.

A few more glasses of wine for you and we were kissing in the smoking shed. I knew then that I had you, and you were the most beautiful girl I had ever seen, you took my breath away.

The next week you were staying late round the flat and then leaving at 2am so that your poor husband didn't suspect anything, but tell me why wasn't that enough. You were keen, keener than I anticipated, and you consumed my every thought. Every text, call and meeting got better and better. You put me first, in front of your husband and kids, so I knew it was real. So tell me, why did you ruin everything? Why did you go back to him and them? How could you do that to me? What had I done to deserve that? We had been through a lot, and then nothing.

You can't just turn me away and pretend I don't exist. You see me and ignore me, you ignore my texts and calls, I wait at the end of the road and you drive past me as if I don't exist.

The times we spent were the best moments of my life and now my life is ruined; if I can't have you, then no one can.

CHAPTER 6

TOLERANCE AND TRUST

I come from a relatively large family, six children in all. I was number five, and my dad would often introduce me as such. We lived in a small council house in the suburbs of London, six children, two adults, living in three bedrooms – it wouldn't be allowed now. The good news was that as there was nearly three years between each sibling, by the time I grew up my elder sisters had left the nest. Still I was sent to boarding school at the age of 11, with my older brother, for five years.

I can't say that my memories were of a super happy house, but similarly I could not complain. I do not remember any dark days, except the time when I was playing football in the house and broke one of my dad's prize aircraft models, and he chased me up the street. I go back to that house sometimes and wonder how we all managed in such a small, cramped dwelling. My conclusion is that we didn't have the time or inclination to complain. Yes, I fought with my brothers and sisters, but it was soon forgotten, there wasn't any space anyway and we weren't exactly rich. The coal man would come every four weeks as we didn't have central heating, the fruit man would deliver boxes of oranges, each orange wrapped separately in tissue paper, and we would use these wrappings as toilet paper. We would take baths once a week to save on electricity which heated the hot water tank and we would walk everywhere. Every material thing was a hand-me-down or from a jumble sale, but we made do.

From 11 to 16 I was sent to a boarding school, all boys, and the five years I spent there made me independent. My older brother's presence was a help and a hindrance. Not everyone liked him, or his classmates, so I would get hassled now and again, but I never got bullied, as there were plenty of other weirdos in my class for anyone to pick on. I was voted most popular class student, something that I was very proud of because my classmates were eclectic to say the least. I was intelligent, which enabled me to befriend the cleverer half of the class, but I was also very good at football, which made me popular with the not so intelligent. Being away from home forced us to keep secrets, from family in particular. I am sure if my dear mother or father knew half the trouble we got in then they would have pulled me out well before the end.

The local town wasn't far from the school, but we had to wear school uniform on every trip, so we were known in the town. We would visit the pubs at the age of 13 and 14, and get served. We would end up in fights with the local teenagers, and win. We would smoke dope in the local park, and no one would say anything, and by the time we were 15, as our hormones were truly established, we were trying to attract the attention of the local girls. Looking back, I think independence has both positive and negative merits; I rarely asked anyone to do anything for me, if I wanted anything or wanted to do anything I would do it myself.

My guess is that this is what shaped me into the person I became. I was patient, very patient, not quick to anger, with a long fuse. I was prudent, which I didn't think was a bad thing. I didn't mind spending money and often wasted a lot, but if I thought I could fix whatever was wrong I would try first, and if I didn't succeed then I would get a man to do it. I preferred to wash the car with the boys rather than pay for the converted BP garage up the road, one of those drive-in car-wash centres, to do it, not to save money but to do something with the boys. I hated throwing away food. She would spend a fortune on a week's shopping, get the ingredients out to make dinner for that evening, demolish a bottle of wine, demand a take away as she couldn't be arsed to cook and then throw away the original food the next morning. To me that was criminal.

I thought I was quite good at most things. Being independent I could iron, hoover, cook, dust, tidy up, make a bed, the list was endless. This became an issue later on in life, because I could do these things my way, to my satisfaction, but I couldn't do any of them to Kate's satisfaction, and it soon became her way or no way. I would hang the laundry in the airing cupboard, only for her to move it all around, saying 'it will dry better like this'. I would stack the dishwasher, only for it to be restacked. I would hang the towels up wrongly, squeeze the toothpaste the wrong way, there no end to my list of faults or inabilities.

After my schooldays came corporate life with various companies headquartered in London, but I was fortunate enough to travel far and wide with work, with a generous expense account. The hedonistic eighties provided much frolics and fun, and girls aplenty. I had a mission, no fear; my friends would look and smile at the girls but I would be the first to go and talk to them. I put them all on some sort of pedestal, probably as I had spent my hormonal years schooling with boys. The alphabet game, to bed the 26 letters of the alphabet, Anna, Bettie, Colleen etc all the way to Zoe, became a raison d'être. I didn't really care about age, height, looks or personality, each girl had a different quality.

I was lucky enough to meet a Polish girl called Iwona, an Irish girl christened Oona and a lady from Armenia named Xhenet. I remember being in a bar after a late lunch meeting a girl called Sandra. I had no interest in her until she told me her name was spelt with a Z, Zandra. I gave up looking for a Q. Most of my twenties were a parody, for boys will be boys. I don't think I knew the word responsible.

My local drinking hole was the Thatched Cottage, a popular place with two bars, one for the oldies with a dartboard, shove ha'penny and round tables. The other bar had a juke box and Space Invader machines, and that was where you would find me; I even had the audacity to bring in my own records and put them on the juke box, although spending money to play a record you have already bought seems a bit frivolous now. The landlord, Deano, called me 'lucky', as there wasn't a month go by without me coming in for a drink with a different partner. He never knew how I did it. I think it was because I respected women, found them interesting, intriguing and infuriating, but I always came back for more. Maybe I respected one or two of them too much; maybe I was too tolerant, too trustworthy. Can you be too trustworthy? They are the ones that ended up hurting me, just desserts.

I wasn't a saint, far from it. I had certainly let people down, broken a few hearts, and I let myself down enough times. As I grew past my thirties I realised that I had to find another path. I had grown into a successful businessman and acquired most things: a wardrobe of expensive suits and ties, a decent flat in a desirable area that overlooked the Thames, a new Porsche Boxster, an ex-wife who didn't bother me and a portfolio of savings that would enable me to retire early, or so I thought.

Then life throws you another curve, and here it was. Kate came into my life on a chance meeting and it turned into our path, our journey, and before long just the two of us became the four us. We shared our lives, all for one, one for all; memories of the past, hope for the future, based on compassion, tolerance and trust.

CHAPTER 7

EXHIBIT 2

Why why why, Kate? You said your husband was shit, you knew he was having an affair, he beat you, he never played with your kids, he hit them, you even suspected he abused them. You said he drank to excess, got angry. You said you had stopped sleeping with him, you needed out. It was killing you living there, that's why we got together, why you wanted to be with me, why you told him that you loved me and were leaving him. You told me that I was the person you were looking for, the only one that understood you for what you are. You said the sex was great - you even bought the Viagra – and lunchtimes were never the same for me. I used to play our favourite songs full blast out of the window so you could hear them from your house. Do you remember Peter Frampton: "woke up this morning with a wine glass in my hand, whose wine what wine, must have been a dream, I don't believe where I've been, come on let's do it again, do you do you feel like I do?" You used to whisper that in my ear as we made love. I bet whenever you hear it you think of me.

You even gave me a key, just in case when he was away I could open the door and catch you in bed. You took my breath and my life away. I was the luckiest man in the world and you made that happen. So why, why, why?

It's been months since I have seen you, talked to you, held you. You must be miserable without me because I know I am without you. I promised I would look after you and your kids, although you said that when you came to live with me he could have them as long as you saw them now and again. We could move, I would sell the house and we could live nearby but not on the same street; if you changed your mind we could fight for custody, I was sure we could win. We could get married on the beach. I wanted to tell the world, people had seen us together and asked. I explained I was in heaven and it was because of you.

Please answer my calls and emails, or send me a letter, tell me you still feel the same. I want to go to the police and tell them that he beats you and the kids are in danger.

There are times when you are not here when I want everything to end. I can't face those quiet times, and just the thought of you coming back keeps me alive. If I ever thought you weren't thinking about me I would kill myself, but first I would make sure you would know.

CHAPTER 8

TWO VIEWS

There was no conversation in the car on the way back to the police station. Detective Inspector Cooper drove slowly back, mulling over his thoughts, whilst Detective Sergeant Leann Stuart scribbled down notes, read the letters proffered and elaborated on issues that she could remember. She underlined various notes and sat back.

When they arrived back at the station they went to the canteen to get some lunch. They both took sandwiches and coffee and retired to a table in the corner, the standard plastic formica top retained the marks and smells of many a lunchtime spill. The chairs were rickety and uncomfortable, but none of this mattered as they took their seats. After a few bites of his cheese and tomato sandwich Cooper started the conversation as Leann knew he would.

'What do you think?' Abrupt and straight to the point.

'Well sir, let's begin with the fact that we haven't heard all the story yet and I am betting there's more to come, and pathology have said that the results won't be in for another two days at least.'

She waited until Cooper gave her a nod; he was interested in what she thought, not the facts.

'My view…' she hesitated as if deciding which way the coin would fall… 'it looks like good love gone bad. I would feel really sorry for our Mr Donaldson but he seemed very composed, maybe even cold, emotionless. I would expect a bit more passion, tears or something.' She waited a while before adding 'in my eyes.'

'Personally, I can't see why he even tried to save the relationship with her. Kate Donaldson seems like a right bitch. Just when he seems to make progress she goes and does something else. I'm surprised he's still got any teeth, he's been kicked in them so many times.' He took another bite of his sandwich. 'If she was mine she would have been out at the first hurdle, being pregnant with someone else's kid on Christmas Day doesn't sound like a foundation for happiness. I'm surprised he didn't throw her out then. The kids seem quite stable and that's because he hides all the fallout from them. He's a saint, if you ask me.'

'They thought Jimmy Savile was a saint a while ago,' said Leann.

Cooper ignored her. 'I agree he seemed emotionless, but I guess he's thinking she committed suicide, and we will still need to confirm that. If that's his thinking then he might even be relieved. In my eyes. I'm wondering why they stayed together. I can see from a traditional old man perspective that he wanted to keep the family together, but if she was that unhappy why didn't she leave? It's not that difficult these days. she didn't seem very motherly. She could have walked out and left him with the kids. What made her so unhappy?

Leann felt that she needed to defend the woman. 'What about if she just felt stuck, didn't want to abandon the kids but didn't have enough money to go it alone, caught between the devil and the deep blue sea? Have you heard of Maslow's hierarchy of needs?'

'Go on, educate me,' he said.

Leann was college educated and had joined the police force after graduating in psychology, whereas

Cooper had been a copper all his life and had worked his way up through the ranks.

'Well it's a theory from development psychology, where there is a physical requirement for us humans. It explains that if these needs are not met then the body cannot function and will ultimately fail. At base it's about air food and water, shelter and self-esteem, leading to self -actualisation - effectively achieve your goals and fulfil your potential.'

'So what has that got to do with this case?'

'Once you achieve your potential you look back on how you got there and what you can do next. Take the analogy of pop stars who fall from grace, footballers who have idiosyncratic personal lives, even politicians and royalty. If you can't handle what you have achieved you may fold, even throw yourself off the summit. It's referred to as Vandell Syndrome. Paul Gascoigne, George Michael, Britney Spears?' Cooper stared blankly. 'Hugh Grant?'

'Yeah, know that one, I get it.'

'Maybe Kate had achieved all she could. As the kids had gone to school, she didn't have to work. She lost her self-esteem, then her focus went and she just threw herself off.'

'Off what?'

'Off the rails, off the cliff, it doesn't matter what, it's the realisation that you can't progress any further.

Lots of victims of this syndrome turn to charity work to keep themselves sane, others give all their riches away. You must have read some celebrity magazines to keep up with what is going on in Hollywood. There's an example of someone going off every month.'

'In my time it was so much simpler. Men and women knew their roles in life.'

Leann let the comment go, knowing Cooper was a bit of a dinosaur. 'It's not only happening to famous people. Imagine if you had been working in Woolworth's, I'm sure you remember them? On the tills for five years, barely minimum wage and had to be careful with your money, then you meet someone who can fend for you. All of a sudden you don't have that need to work, or be prudent, you can just spend and do what you want. After a while you can go crazy because you've lost that basic instinct for "need", hence the hierarchy of need. You have too much time on your hands and don't know what to do.'

'Sounds a bit like Pygmalion,' offered Cooper.

'Yes and no. In Pygmalion a low-esteemed individual is encouraged to better herself by building her self-esteem, rather successfully, so successfully in fact that there is a phenomenon studied called the Pygmalion effect. However the Vandell syndrome is based on the individual. It's not built up or encouraged but rather just put on that pedestal, just planked there. Do you see the difference?'

Cooper nodded. 'Any other not-so-intellectual theories?'

'Alternatively he got fed up with her and decided to do something about it. I really want to see what else is going to come out. We always look for motive and if pathology or toxicology come back with anything then I guess we have a motive, quite a strong one.'

'Motive my ass. He's had to put up with this for years for his kids, why would he do anything now? Let's spend this afternoon with that list. We can get some plods to help and we will ask for his computer tomorrow as a matter of course after we get the next chapter of this saga. I hope it's not as bad as the first, for his sake.'

'But sir, the Jeremy Kyle show has this saga every day. It happens to everyone. Relationships break down as a fact of life and people do things to protect themselves, going out having affairs, drinking. It's a cry for help. I understand her, a bit. She couldn't leave and she couldn't stay. And women are different from men.'

'I know that,' snorted Cooper. 'Just ask the wife.'

There were a few minutes' silence as Cooper finished his lunch.

'What do you make of the letters?' he asked.

'You mean the content of the letters, or the letters themselves?'

'Good question. Why not give me your opinion on both? I haven't read them yet.'

'Ok, firstly the letters. Two things struck me straight away – why did she keep them and why did he photocopy them? The second I can understand, because if he was thinking about a custody case he has some solid evidence rather than hearsay, but I still don't know why she kept them. At the moment it doesn't sound like a fantastic memento of the past. As for the content, it's pretty safe stuff, a few personal comments but no explicit threats or such. However there is some implicit "you can't leave me" stuff, and we don't even know how this Kevin fits in yet.'

'Let's keep them under wraps for the time being, we can always go back and use them as reference if we need to,' suggested Cooper.

'Sure. Just one last thing, I've been thinking, I wonder what else he found?'

CHAPTER 9

ANOTHER STEP DOWN

We spent the spring and early summer coming to terms with each other. We talked about not splitting up, keeping together, how we needed each other, how the kids needed us and how we could build a future. I was working during the week and she was at work most weekends, looking after old people; the boys were at school. The days were passing by, the cracks over our relationship were being papered over slowly, normality was returning.

Then the lure of the lunchtime pub, the company and the booze got to her again. We went from content to contempt in six months.

The first major disaster was when I took the boys to our caravan in Dorset for the weekend. She had started working as a personal assistant to an old guy, Charles, who lived four doors down, a curmudgeon of a man who needed two visits a day, lunch, dinner, medication, cleaning, ironing all that, and at weekends she also worked on a carer round that took her out in the evenings till around ten. So during the week she would go around to Charles house in the morning and spend a couple of hours and then between 6pm and eightish she would do the evening call; she was enjoying looking after him. On Saturdays she would do a round from 7am till 11am and then out from 5pm till 10pm. Charles liked her and even had a birthday party when he invited her and some friends around. The boys and I couldn't go as we had booked the caravan for the weekend. I got a call on the Saturday afternoon saying she was at Charles's lunchtime and then was going off to work later that evening; I reminded her not to drink as she was driving.

I rang her mobile that evening, as I hadn't managed to speak to her earlier in the afternoon, but didn't get a response. I tried again several times, and eventually she answered and tried to tell me she was sitting in a car waiting for her next appointment. She was slurring her speech and I couldn't hear her properly, with music and general noise in the background. She hung up and called me back a couple of minutes later. She was clearly pissed. It was still noisy, so I asked again what she was doing and got the same story. I left it at that and got a voicemail about 1am saying she loved me, but the rest was garbled. I tried to make out what she was saying several times, but the words didn't make sentences. I went to bed with a heavy feeling in my chest. I considered returning home to check she was OK, I tossed and turned, unable to sleep and wondering what was coming next.

The next morning the boys and I left the caravan early and drove home as fast as was legally possibly, including some parts of the motorway where our speed was definitely not legally possible. When we arrived at our house we hurried into the lounge. It was about 11am, and she was drunk and looked an absolute mess. Her eyes were still rolling and it was obvious she had had a heavy night. I even thought she might have been taking something, cocaine maybe? This wasn't just alcohol induced, even a blind man could see that.

The boys and I unpacked and I prepared lunch for them. I then sent them upstairs to play, as even though they had only been gone a day from the house they missed their Xbox. I sat down next to her and asked her what had she been doing, where had she been, what had she taken. She said she had had a few drinks but had gone to work in the evening and fallen asleep as soon as she'd come home, then phoned me when she'd woken up. I didn't believe her and asked her to swear on the boys' lives, which she duly did. What else can you do? You have to accept someone's word if they swear on their children's lives, don't you?

This really bugged me; after we had been through so much I knew something was wrong. She got aggressive later that day, accusing me of not believing her and asking what I thought she had done. She even suggested I should ring a colleague of hers who would tell me where they had worked that evening. I decided against this course of action and hoped that whatever had happened would just disappear. I knew she was lying. I had had enough of this, this was the start of a downward spiral, a real step change, for her, for us, for the children and life in general.

Looking after Charles became a routine. She would walk the four houses down the road to Charles's every morning about 10am, fix him some lunch, pop back at 2pm and then go back again at 6pm to take his dinner round. It was cash in hand and paying more than she had earned in a while, and she really enjoyed looking after Charles in the beginning.

His next-door neighbour was Kevin, who was older than me, just retired, lived on his own and had spent several years looking after Charles as a friendly neighbour. We had met him several times and we often chatted about work. He had been in a similar field to me and seemed friendly enough, although some other neighbours didn't get on with him, I never knew why. It transpired that Kevin and Charles would have a gin and tonic in the morning, open a bottle of wine at lunchtime and then some evenings Kevin would go round later and open another bottle. He had a lot of time on his hands and Charles was an interesting person.

To Kate this was an ideal escape from the boredom of being a housewife. I was working and used to come home about five to find her pissed on the settee, often asleep with the kids amusing themselves. She was functioning at a manic level. She would clean and tidy the house before 10am so that she could go round to Charles's house. She would have a gin and tonic, and then at lunchtime she would join them with a bottle of wine, but it was in the evenings that the problems started. It quickly went from 'I am taking Charles's dinner round and might stop for one drink', to staying for three hours and returning home legless after the kids had gone to bed. I got into the bad habit of calling and telling her to come home and she got into the habit of not answering her phone.

There was one night when for some reason she brought Kevin back to our house. I had gone to bed, the kids were asleep and she and Kevin started playing music downstairs. After a while I went down to see what was going on. They were in each other's space, both pissed, laughing and smoking in the kitchen. As politely as I could I kicked him out; she was furious. The next day she told me to go round and apologise to him, which I did. He said something like 'she is very attractive and you should watch her', to which I replied something about beauty being on the inside.

The nights out became more frequent, the duration longer, and the kids were getting upset. They even stood at the door begging her not to go out, but she just brushed past them and walked out. In her lucid moments she told me she and Kevin were just friends and she needed adult conversation and what was wrong with me, was I jealous? Did I really think that she was sleeping with a 68-year-old pensioner?

We had arranged a holiday, and the night before we were due to depart she went round Kevin's. She wasn't late home as we had to get up early to catch the flight. It was late spring and it had been a lovely day, turning into a quiet evening. She went to bed and I followed up shortly after. Three doors down, Kevin had cranked up his stereo. I had noticed several times that

I could hear his music, but hadn't really registered it. This time Pete Frampton was on a loop singing 'Do you feel the way I do...' It struck me as a strange song; I understand now that he wanted her to hear it. That song stuck with me all night, running through the middle of my head like a freight train.

She had told me that she had left Kevin a key to the house, just in case, and whilst we were away she phoned him several times to check on the house.

Our week away in the sun didn't turn out as I had expected. I was looking forward to time with the family, four of us on the beach, walks to lovely restaurants by the sea and a romantic quiet time after Luke and Taylor had gone to bed. I had suggested we get a hotel as the boys would have company and maybe we could get some free time, just the two of us, but she booked a private villa in the hills. Instead of peace and tranquillity, I spent a week playing with the boys in the swimming pool, playing pool in the games house, playing football, tennis, taking the boys to the beach, the demands were endless. I couldn't complain as I always enjoy playing with them, but you only want to hear 'Dad, can you...?' so many times in a day, and when there are two of them, it is even more demanding.

Kate lazed around, drinking lager in the sun until lunchtime, when she would hit the wine. The evenings became argument after argument over nothing, and I ended up sleeping with one of the boys every night whilst she had taken the other into the main bedroom.

The day we got home the first job was to dump the clothes out of the suitcases into the washing pile and get started with the chores of post-holiday tidying. When I took the empty suitcases upstairs to put them away, I noticed that some of her cupboards were open and the bed had been turned down; I was sure that wasn't the way we'd left it. Her underwear drawer was open and it appeared that it had been riffled through. I called her upstairs and asked what she thought. She dismissed it quickly and said she had done it before she left, and no one had been in the house. That struck me as strange, as I hadn't asked that question. In the fridge were a few bottles of wine, her favourite Pinot but a different brand from her usual choice. I didn't know how they had got there.

The next month things got worse. Sometimes she would take the kids round in the evenings to Kevin's, where they would play on his computer, eat sweets and generally mess around. One time I had taken our eldest to football, and when we got home no one was in. I called, and she was round at Kevin's. I asked her to come home, which she did about an hour later on her own, having left Taylor at Kevin's house. We were arguing in the garden, as she swore that she had not left him there, when Kevin walked up the road holding Taylor's hand. My son let go of his hand, ran towards me and after a kiss and cuddle hurried into our house to see his brother, exclaiming that they should have gone together to Kevin's as he had been eating chocolate all evening. She thanked Kevin in front of me, put her arm around his neck and kissed him on the lips. I swear he winked at me before he turned and left. I didn't move. I didn't believe what I had just seen; maybe I just imagined it. This image became indelibly printed on my brain.

I glared at her and walked into the house, debating whether to say something about it, but just didn't have the strength to do so. Some things you don't want hear. Some things you don't want to see.

I had to go to America with work for three nights and told her she had to stay sober, as it was the boys' half term, and she promised she would. When I called home the next day she told me about her day, how she had taken the kids for lunch and left her car at the pub. Kevin had collected it for her later, so he was round the house playing with the kids. The next day I called again and Kevin was round again. I spoke to my sons about what they had been doing, and they said they had been down the pub with Kevin all day and then watched a DVD around his house. Kevin had helped bath them and they told me it was real fun as he was jumping up and down on the bed making them laugh. I asked them to put their mum back on the phone, which they did. I asked what was going on and she told me that Kevin and his sister had come round, so it wasn't as if Kevin was there on his own. The boys hadn't mentioned Kevin's sister – I never knew he had one. As they said goodnight I asked if Kevin had been there on his own, and they both said yes, only Kevin.

I felt our lives were not going to plan, well my plan at least, and there was nothing I could do about it.

On my return I asked about Kevin, as I thought it was strange that he had spent all that time around my house. She swore again that there was nothing going on, and when I mentioned Kevin coming round on his own she initially told me that the boys had been lying, insisting his sister had been with him. Even in front of the boys she told both of them they were lying about Kevin's sister. This was very disturbing. How can you accuse your own children of lying to save yourself? I approached the same subject a week later when she was sober and relatively lucid, and she admitted that Kevin didn't have a sister but said nothing had happened and she had only told me that story so that I wouldn't be worried or start accusing her of having an affair.

We sat down and I suggested she should start seeing a therapist. Her drinking was out of control and

I was not qualified to deal with this. I was really worried about the kids, as whenever she went out they wanted to phone her and ask her what time she was coming home, just in case she never did. There were times where she would come home, kiss the kids goodnight and go out again, and I knew this wasn't good.

Not being an idiot, I decided I need some proof. This was driving me mad. I couldn't work, I was getting depressed and my blood pressure was going through the roof. One evening, Kevin had some friends over and she asked me if she could she go round, saying she wouldn't be home late. It must have been after 11pm when I crept out of the house, walked down the towpath and hid behind the hedge adjacent to Kevin's house, from which I had a good view of the front room and kitchen through the windows not 10 yards away. I was sure I couldn't be seen.

Music was playing and a few people were dancing. Kate was dancing on her own; I couldn't see Kevin. When she dances she is one of the sexiest women I have seen, and that was what I was thinking when Kevin came into the room with two glasses of wine, put them down and then leaned over and kissed her tenderly.

I was mad. I wanted to bang on the window, or smash it. I didn't know what to do, and this was all going on in front of people I had met. I stumbled back down the towpath and heaved, but nothing came up. I leaned against the bush to steady myself, my heart racing and sat there seething. She never came home that night, said she'd fallen asleep on the settee and I had nothing to worry about. I didn't tell her I had seen her.

The next week it happened again. It was late and she still wasn't home, so I hid behind the same hedge and Kate was sitting on the kitchen table. I could see clearly. Kevin came to her, she opened her legs and he reached behind her, stroking the back of her neck, and they kissed; this time I did kick off. I jumped out from behind the bush and strode towards the window. I banged loudly, nearly breaking the glass and shouted at both of them, and they opened the kitchen door. Kevin looked sheepish, like he had been caught with his hand in the cookie jar. She – well, she was drunk, eyes like pissholes in the snow, but she was defiant, trying to be all self-righteous, looking at me as if she was wondering what the hell I thought I was doing. I didn't know what to do and told her to get home, and she said she didn't want to. I stormed off and went home, and she followed ten minutes later. As always she went on the offensive, demanding to know what was I doing leaving the kids on their own and saying she was going to report me to social services! It was all in my imagination, she had had a very controlling boyfriend when she was younger and now I was trying to control her. How could I even think of suggesting that she was having sex with Kevin? What proof did I have? She swore on the kids' lives that nothing was happening. I think I had heard that before.

I don't know how I didn't hit her there and then. I think I was worried that if I hit her I wouldn't stop. If you want a reason to kill someone then that was it, she was driving me mad. I turned on my heels and went to bed.

CHAPTER 10

TRUTH DAY

After two days of not talking, we sat down again. I wanted to know what was going on. She told me nothing was going on, but she agreed that her drinking had got out of hand. I insisted that something had to be done, we couldn't live like this. She blamed me for fuelling the kid's brains with hatred, because they had started asking Mummy not to go out and not to drink.

She picked a local therapist specialising in alcohol and depression from an Internet search and arranged an appointment. At first she would tell me about her sessions, what was said, how the therapist agreed that I was controlling, how it was my fault that she drank as I didn't trust her, how the kids were taking my side because I was telling them to.

I looked at myself. I was sure I wasn't going mad, but I was concerned, really concerned, and didn't know what I could do. Did I make her drink? If I didn't trust her as I thought she wasn't trustworthy, was I being fair? Had I ever told the boys anything bad about their mum? I didn't believe I had, I wanted them to love her and feel loved by her, just the same as I wanted.

Days came and days went, and I lived my life walking on eggshells in the day. The music from Kevin's stereo haunted me at night, playing songs of love and affection; was it a coincidence that every night she stayed in, the music would start as if she was being serenaded?

Summer had started and the kids were due to break up for the summer holidays in a couple of weeks, but Kate started getting manic again. I know why now, because with the boys at home she couldn't play away, though I didn't know that then. She was back having a few drinks at lunchtime and walking to pick the kids up instead of driving. This wasn't an issue until she started turning up at school later and later, and the kids would tell me that they had to wait for her. This wasn't on. I sat her down and explained that this was unacceptable, and she promised it wouldn't happen again. This generated a bigger problem, because out of the blue the boys told me that Kevin picked them up sometimes and Mummy had told them not to say anything. I had taken a couple of days off, working from home, so I went to get them myself As I was standing outside the school gates, some of the mums and dads seemed a bit off to me, but I didn't take much notice. One of the mothers approached me and told me that if my wife ever turned up drunk again in the car to pick the kids up she would call the police, as it was too dangerous. She was genuinely worried about the children, hers and mine; if your wife wants to kiss her boyfriend in the car at the school gates, can she make sure that her own kids do not see what's going on, as they have started asking questions.

I was shocked and agreed that she should call the police if they saw her drink-driving again. I didn't know what to say, I felt ashamed and was wondering what the kids at school were saying to my children.

We had a massive argument that night. I knew I shouldn't have had a drink beforehand but I think I was at tipping point. She stormed out. It was all lies, she claimed, the other mums were jealous because she was still pretty whilst they had let themselves go. She said she wasn't having an affair, but the way I was going she might consider it. She stormed out and didn't get back until the next morning, and then the first thing she did was open a bottle of wine. I kept out of the way, and took the kids to school. I knew that if I went home after school I would kill her; instead I went out for the day and tried to clear my head.

It was a couple of days later when in one of her more lucid moments I sat down with her and told her that she had got herself in a hole and couldn't get out. The more lies you tell the harder it is to tell the truth, and it becomes a vicious circle. She listened, then went into the kitchen and poured a glass of wine and explained that on the kids' lives nothing had happened. The therapist was helping her and if I could just stay patient, everything would be fine.

The next week the kids were due to break up on the Friday. On the Thursday when I came home from work, she had unknown to me arranged for the boys to stay at a friend's house after school for a while. I didn't know I was walking into a storm. As I pulled into the drive she was sitting on the doorstep with a small bag packed and the inevitable glass of wine in one hand. She was pissed and it was 3pm.

She told me to sit down and said 'you want the truth, I'll tell you the truth and then I am leaving.' I realised that I was going to hear something I didn't want to, again.

She told me she had been sleeping with Kevin for the past three months, her choice. She had even bought Viagra for him; whilst I was away Kevin came round on his own every night, not just the once. She loved Kevin, and he didn't criticise her for drinking or ask her to stop. He accepted her as she was. She was moving out and she would tell the kids tomorrow.

She pushed past me. 'I never loved you. Now you know what you wanted to know, are you happy? And by the way, just in case you hear it from someone else, I was also sleeping with Nick until the last couple of months, but the good news is I am not pregnant.'

My instinct was to grab her, but my arms wouldn't work. My mouth opened but nothing came out. I just stood there dazed as she walked out of the garden and through the gates and turned right towards Kevin's house. At least if she was not here I couldn't kill her.

I remembered this as Truth Day.

The secrets that we shared,
The mountains that we moved,
Caught like a wildfire out of control,
Till there was nothing left to burn or nothing left to prove
And I remember what she said to me,
How she swore that it never would end,
I remember how she held me so tight,
Wish I don't know now what I didn't know then,
Against the wind, we were running against the wind.

Looks like I'm not going to work for a while.

CHAPTER 11

EXHIBIT 3

Hey it's me, I had to go away for a while, couldn't stop thinking about you but it's done no good. I hope you think of me as much. I understand you got problems but I can fix them for you. I know what you like, I dropped some stuff of at your place, I hope you got it, when your head is full have some and think of me and our time together, maybe that will help you see what you missed most about us. Then dream about us being together and I will make it happen. You only have to call once and I will come running and save you from that horrible life that you have. I still don't understand why you left, but that doesn't matter any more because I know we will be together shortly.

I was thinking of that night when my friend came round, just the three of us; that was wild, real wild, you took so much and smiled all the way through it. I knew you would like it, didn't have to talk you into it too much, are you sure that you don't want to do that again? Anytime you want I will be here for you, just call me.

CHAPTER 12

THE BOYS

Luke and Taylor were inseparable. Like all siblings they fought and bickered, but they also protected and cherished each other. Before the fatal 'truth day', she and I had spent several months arguing. The Christmas episode had been underwritten – I mean a line had been drawn under it – and she wasn't seeing Nick any more, or so I thought, and she had started working at Charles's house. Luke and Taylor were eight and seven respectively. The step change when she started drinking at Charles's with Kevin became a family affair.

The boys looked similar, blonde hair and blue eyes, same as their dad, but were very different in build and temperament. Luke was big, the tallest boy in his class, something his dad never was, while Taylor was small - not the smallest, but slight and nifty as opposed to his older brother, who was strong and sturdy. Luke was into football, playing as goalkeeper for a local team and training three times a week. He was competitive to a fault. He didn't like losing at anything and would often throw a strop if he wasn't winning at cards, chess or tennis – he would declare the game was over and walk off. Taylor was so much more laid back. He could play football but he did not really care about the score, he just enjoyed himself.

Luke was constantly seeking attention and did not like being on his own, whilst Taylor was quite happy sitting playing with his 'Skylanders' or other characters and did not need constant company.

As they grew, the differences between them grew. Luke's favourite word became 'no' and Taylor's was 'why?', and both words infuriated me. I think I did so much for them, but they were not grateful. I got angry, occasionally, but most of the time I was very patient with them. I had my own rules - do not swear at them, do not tell either of them to shut up, try and entertain them whenever I can. Sometimes I think I went too far in putting the boys first.

In her lucid moments, Kate would tell me that I was the best father they could ever have, which made me proud. She told me that she had missed a lot of the kids growing up; she had physically there but not involved. I was the one who took them out, I was the one they called for in the middle of the night, I was the one who went to the school plays. She wished she had spent more time with them.

The family affair became a real cause of concern. For Luke the dramas were played out in full in front of him and he got involved; Taylor stood back and hid away from any confrontation. It was Luke, aged eight, in his school uniform of blue polo shirt and grey shorts, who stood in the hallway screaming for us to stop arguing as she was walking out of the door to go and see Kevin. It was Luke who would ask 'where is Mummy, can I call her? Is she coming home tonight?' It was Luke who saw me crying several times and couldn't understand why.

I remember coming home with the boys from school. I had finished work and texted her to say I could pick them up; I didn't get a reply, and she wasn't in when we got home. I didn't know where she was, but I guessed she was round Charles's. I called a few times and left messages for her but to no avail, so after about an hour I started making the boys dinner. She turned up as I had put the food in the cooker, wanting to know what I was doing – did I really think she wouldn't be home to feed the kids? Why was I making her out to be a bad mother? At these times I would argue back, but the accusations were so absurd to me that I didn't have much to say.

She was shaking uncontrollably and said she was going out for a walk. Luke stepped in and asked her not to go, and she told him she would be 10 minutes, but he didn't believe her. It wouldn't be the first time she had gone for 10 minutes and come back the next morning. I asked her not to go as well, and then Taylor arrived to see what was going on

'Piss off, just piss off all of you!' she shouted. 'You make me go, I hate you all, just leave me alone, if I want to go out I will, you can't stop me!'

Luke stood in the doorway between the kitchen and hall. 'Please don't go 'he pleaded, with his arms and legs stretched out wide to make a barrier, tears rolling down his cheeks.

'Just fuck off, I'm out of here, you are all a bunch of shits, you think I am a bad mum, I'll show you!' She picked up Luke and removed him from the doorway. 'I was going to be back by eight but now I just might stay out all night.' Then she stumbled out of the door.

Luke was in tears and Taylor joined in, although I

don't think he knew why he was crying. I put dinner on hold and sat down, cradling them in my arms.

Luke wanted to know, why does Mummy get like that, why does she swear at me? Taylor just sobbed. After a while I made pizzas for them, gave them an ice cream and took them up for a bath. The en-suite bathroom is adjacent to the main bedroom, and as they were sitting in the bath Luke looked over and saw me crying on the bed, tears rolling down my cheeks, but no sound. I remember seeing him looking at me and I feeling that I was the child and he was the parent.

Luke and I had several moments throughout these months when we consoled each other, looking for answers, solutions and reasons. We came up with none.

She must have got in early one morning, as I heard the door open and the crash and clanging of wine bottle being taken from the fridge. I came downstairs in the morning and she was asleep on the settee. I made breakfast and was bringing the boys down to get ready for school when she woke up and wondered what I was doing, claiming it was 7pm not 7am and asking why the boys were going to school in the evening. I sent them to get washed and dressed and asked her what was going on. She told me that she had been at Charles all afternoon and evening and fell asleep on a chair around Charles. I explained that she had come home, and we had a big argument. She did not remember coming home, she told me I was making it up just to make her look bad. Luke stepped in, he had been listening, and he told her that she had come home and pushed him to get out of the door. She looked at him and told him that he was lying as well, then got up and went up to bed. She never apologised for this. She used to say, 'Why would I apologise for something I don't remember?'

I sat down with Luke several times, as these episodes were getting more frequent. I tried to explain that Mummy wasn't well, Mummy was tired, Mummy didn't mean to say these things; I have no idea how an eight-year-old could assimilate or understand what was happening or if what I said to him was placating him in any way.

Taylor was different. I sat down with him too, but he seemed oblivious to what was happening. Maybe he was too young, or maybe he just kept his feelings inside.

I cannot claim that their behaviour changed due to the atmosphere at home, though I can recall Luke telling me to piss off, shut the fuck up and other combinations at various times when he was not getting his own way. I let it ride sometimes and then later I would sit him down and talk to him, explaining that I didn't swear and I would like him to be like his father.

His response was 'If Mummy can say that to you, why can't I?' Typical Luke. He understood what was happening, he understood that Kevin was a threat to his home, he thought that to get his own way he needed to swear and shout, like his mother.

Taylor was a different animal; he began arguing with his mother more than me. The simplest request would descend into a fight because he would respond with 'Why do you want me to do this?', 'Why don't you do it yourself?', 'Why should I?' It was as if he was responding to her thoughts rather than her actions or words. He had no realisation of actions and consequences, but it was difficult to tell him off as he did not care, he lived for the now.

After Truth Day the boys settled down. Luke remembered the bad times and we used to talk about them, but Taylor just remembered having fun around Kevin's.

CHAPTER 13

THE FALLOUT

The officers turned up on time, and I opened the door and invited them in. They walked through the hall, with its canvas prints of Luke, Taylor and their mum. I led them through the lounge, where the open fire was burning gently, just taking the nip out of the air; although the windows that faced the river provided a fantastic view, they also caused a nasty draught. We went into the kitchen and sat back down at the table where we had started the day before.

They were both dressed in very businesslike fashion; I think they call that 'smart casual'. They sat down at the table and accepted the tea I had made them. I had remembered the sugar and milk, but they took no sugar.

They started going over a few details. They both had typed copies of the list of people I had provided yesterday and I could see notes attached to most of them; they must have been the ones they tracked down last night, so they had been busy.

They asked for both computers, which I duly provided. I knew there was nothing on mine, and although I had searched hers a few weeks earlier I had left no path of detection. I had left a few inappropriate web links on mine, as I didn't want to appear holier than thou, and I do like people to think I am normal. The questions from yesterday's interview had been more fundamental than investigative, a few dates needing confirming, details on the car accident (that was an easy one for them to confirm), and some background on family and friends, and I duly obliged to the best of my ability. They asked about Luke and Taylor, and how they were coping. I replied, 'The kids are doing as well as can be expected, but thanks for asking'.

After about 10 minutes of pleasantries, Cooper looked at Leann and I saw a small nod which I understood to mean 'let's start talking'. She asked me if I wanted to add anything from yesterday, and if not to carry on as before, wherever I saw fit to start.

So I started on Kevin – well, about him. I started talking about the last 12 months, starting with the good times, going over the fallout from the trip to the caravan and concluding on the night the truth had come out. It lasted about an hour and half. There were a few points where I had to stop as I remembered the bad times, but basically I kept myself under control.

As I told my story I was assessing them. Cooper seemed to be the typical copper, doing everything by the book and listening intently to dates and timelines; Leann was more intuitive, picking up on different nuances, slightly disbelieving, wanting to know how I had felt rather than what I had done.

She interrupted me at one stage. 'Thank you for all this, but besides the letters do you have any other proof that any of this happened?'

I stopped and thought, looked through my notes on the table and pulled out an A4 page which I had printed out that morning.

'I'm not sure what proof I can show you. I didn't take photographs, I hardly talked to anyone, it wasn't something I wanted to share, except with the therapist, but I did write this down the day after it happened. You can check my PC to see what date it was written.'

I handed it over so she could read it, and Cooper pulled his chair closer to Leann so he could read it over her shoulder.

I got up, stretched my legs and left them. I knew every line by heart.

CHAPTER 14

A DAY IN THE LIFE

I got a text at lunchtime: could I pick the boys up from school, she was busy working around Charles's and wanted to finish something. I left the office in London at 1pm, caught the train home and picked my car up from the local railway station car park. It was 2:30pm when I arrived at the school car park, and I hung around the gates as usual talking to other mums and dads; the boys would be out at 3pm. We loaded the car up and came straight home, listening to music on the

CD player. They were both in high spirits, telling stories from their day.

When we got home, their mum's car was there but there was no sign of her in the house. The boys called out greetings but got no response. I picked up the post from the floor and dropped the letters onto my desk in the office. I unpacked their bags, tidied up and put them away. She had obviously had something to eat that morning as the frying pan was in the sink and plates were left on the worktop. I cleaned the kitchen and then went into the laundry room, where the washing machine was buzzing away. The boys had gone upstairs to play, and I emptied the washing machine and hung the clothes up in the boiler room to dry. I unpacked my stuff and set my PC up in the office to check my emails. I flicked through the post; nothing unusual or unexpected.

I texted her to see what time she would be back and got an immediate response that she would be home to make the boys their dinner at the usual time, 4:30. The boys and I messed around until about 5pm, still no show, so I called and left a voicemail. I texted, still no response. I made the boys their dinner, chicken nuggets and chips, and called them down to eat.

Half way through their dinner she strode into the house and said hello to the boys. I was in the kitchen. I turned around to see that she was wearing a white summer dress and pumps, and her blonde hair was drawn back into a pony tail. She was wearing large sunglasses, although it wasn't sunny. On her dress there were what looked like splatters of red wine.

'What the fuck are you looking at?' she said. Not a great way to start a conversation.

'I wasn't looking at anything' I answered, rather defensively.

'Don't fucking start, I had a drink around Charles's house, what is wrong with that?'

'I haven't said anything.'

She pushed past me, put down her bag, plugged in her mobile, and got herself a glass of wine from the fridge. Her hands were shaking and the wine spilt on the kitchen floor as she went back into the lounge, put the television on and flopped onto the settee.

'I told you I was going to be back to make the kids' dinner, why didn't you wait?' she shouted through the open door.

'They said they were hungry, I did text and call you.'

'Yeah, you always text and call me, why can't you just make a decision yourself, what's wrong with you? Is it too difficult to make dinner for these little shits?'

I went quiet and carried on tidying up the kitchen. Then I took the boys' cleared plates and drink cups to the dishwasher and sent them upstairs to play before bath time.

'Whilst you are in the kitchen you can make some dinner for Charles, there is a ready meal in the fridge,' she said.

'OK.' I tried to sound cheery. I microwaved a mashed potato and beef stew ready meal, took it out, rested it for a minute then transferred it to a plate. Nearly every day she cooked Charles a meal and took it round about six. I covered the plate with cling film and left it on the worktop. When I walked past her she had changed the television channel and was watching Jeremy Kyle. She still had her sunglasses on, and I knew she was pissed.

I went in to the office and continued to catch up on stuff that I hadn't done because I had left work early. She got up to go for a smoke outside and had to walk past the office.

'Have you emptied the washing machine? Leave the ironing, I'll do it later. Why are you always on that fucking computer, you live on it, why don't you do something with the kids?'

I ignored the comments. I didn't want another fight.

On her return journey she shouted out as she walked past, 'You can take Charles's dinner round, I can't be arsed.'

It was quiet for the next 20 minutes. I went to get a drink from the kitchen and her phone buzzed, incoming text I guessed. She jumped up, hurriedly picked her phone up and went back to the settee. She read her text and started drumming her fingers on the keyboard in a response.

'Right' I called, 'I will take Charles's dinner round.'

'What for? I always do it, are you trying to tell me I'm too drunk to take his fucking dinner round? "

'No, you just asked me to.'

'I fucking didn't, you think I am mental or something? I am taking it round.'

I didn't answer. I had heard the same comment several times. One time I had explained that I didn't think she was mental but she needed help, and this had descended into a massive argument.

Taylor heard the shouting and came downstairs. 'What's up?'

'Nothing sweaty' she answered. 'I'm just taking Charles's dinner round.'

'Please don't go Mummy, you said we could all watch a film tonight.'

'I will only be five minutes, I promise.'

'No you won't, you said that last night and we didn't see you.'

'I will, I promise, if I'm not back in five minutes you can call me. No, make that fifteen minutes.' She picked up the plate, her phone and her handbag and waddled to the door. I didn't say anything.

To cheer the boys up we played cards for half an hour, then as a special treat they had a bath together. At 7pm I called her; I had left it an hour, no response, I left a voicemail pointing out that she had promised she would be back in 15 minutes. With the boys bathed, pyjamas on and sitting in front of the television, we went to put the film on.

'Mum's not here, can I call her?' asked Luke.

'Of course.' I handed my mobile to him and he dialled.

'She's not there, can I try again?'

He did so, three times, no answer. I suggested that maybe her phone wasn't working and we could try again later.

We watched *Men in Black* and they enjoyed it thoroughly, even though they had seen it twice before. It was 9pm when the film had finished, and I made supper.

'Time for bed' I said.

'Can we wait for Mummy? or can I call her?'

'Sure.' I phoned and she answered.

'What the fuck do you want? Why have you called me five times? Are the kids dead? What's the urgency?'

I kept calm.

'I am putting the boys to bed and they were wondering if you were coming home to say goodnight.'

'What you doing that for? S'only seven o'clock.' She

was angry and her slurred words were hard to understand,

'No, it's just gone nine.'

'Tell them I'll be home in fifteen minutes, to say goodnight, and don't call again.'

We waited, watching television for 30 minutes.

'Boys we have to go to bed now, you have school tomorrow.' They were both tired by now. 'I know what, I'll tell you a story.'

That seemed to work. They ran upstairs and got into bed.

Sometimes we played a game where they would choose a subject and a situation and I would have to invent a story on the hoof. Tonight it was a devil on an aeroplane. Not easy, especially when your head is about to burst with all the thoughts going through your mind.

Eventually their heads hit the sack, and they were soon snoring gently. Downstairs I tidied up; it was getting near 10pm. I realised that I still hadn't taken my work suit off. I started getting school bags ready for the next day; they had no shirts or trousers ready so I did the ironing, got myself something to eat and went upstairs, turning all the lights off. I got into bed. There was nothing I could do; I felt an absolute failure.

I put the radio on low. A talk show programme was discussing the effect on children of abusive and alcoholic fathers. Married mothers and single mothers were calling in with their tales of woe and hardship, but not one father called in to describe the other side of the coin. Was it just me?

I finally fell asleep but a short time later, something woke me up. I looked at the alarm clock on the bedside table: 2:10am. I could hear someone trying to get in through the front door. Then it went quiet; the door hadn't opened. I went downstairs and opened it. She was sitting on the step with her key in hand, handbag over her shoulder and shoes left strewn on the path. She stood up slowly and said. 'What the fuck you doing up? You checking on me? Why did you lock the door?'

She pushed past me, weaved her way into the lounge, slammed the door and put the television on. I went outside and brought in her shoes, then I shut and locked the door and went back upstairs.

I tried to sleep. I could hear her banging around in the kitchen; a glass smashed and the television was turned up. After about an hour I came back downstairs. She was asleep, snoring on the settee. I turned the television down and went into the kitchen. I cleaned up the glass on the floor, turned the hob and oven off. She had obviously started to make herself something to eat and then crashed, leaving everything on. I turned the lights off in the kitchen and lounge, found a kid's blanket and draped it over her. Her handbag was open on the carpet and her bra was in the handbag; that's odd, I thought. I left the television on low and went back to bed; I had work in the morning.

It was 6am when my alarm started buzzing. I went downstairs and found her awake watching the news, a can of cider in her hand. I walked past her and put the kettle on. I went back into the lounge, promising myself that I wouldn't start a fight.

'What was that all about last night?' I asked calmly.

'If you've got something to say just fucking say it, or grow up.'

I never understood how an argument start and finish in one sentence.

'Do you remember what happened last night?' I asked.

'Course I fucking do, I went to Charles's at lunchtime and didn't come home till 11pm, and I checked my phone I had 7 missed calls, where do you think I was? He's 91 years old. I fell asleep on his settee, that's why I didn't answer your calls. What is your problem?'

I took a deep breath and told her what had actually happened. She didn't remember coming home at tea time, she didn't remember promising the boys she would be straight back, she didn't remember talking to them later in the evening, she didn't remember me at the door at 2am. She had no recollection of leaving the hob and oven on, or of any broken glass.

'So, nobody died. Can't you look after the kids for one night? Are you that fucking stupid?'

I walked out and went upstairs for a shower; there was nothing I could say. On my return she was already into can number two.

'Haven't you gone to work yet?' she said.

'No, I need to take the kids to school as you obviously can't drive in that state.'

'What fucking state is that?' She rose from the settee and stood in my space, face to face. 'You are nothing but a worthless piece of shit, I hate you, are you taking the fucking shits to school just to make me out to be a bad mother? Why is it always my fault? You need to seriously take a look at yourself before you blame me, you cunt. I am going to bed. Do not wake me.'

With that she took her can of cider, stormed out the room and slammed the door shut. I never had a chance to ask where she had been, what she had she been doing or why her bra was in her handbag. I felt so alone.

Within an hour, I had the boys fed, washed, dressed and ready for school. They wanted to say good bye to Mummy, so we crept to the top of the stairs and whispered goodbye. I led them out of the front door and they ran off to get into the car. I slowly closed the door behind me so as not to wake her and stood on the doorstep. I knew I had forgotten something.

'Come on Dad, we'll be late for school!'

I remembered then. It was my birthday. Happy Fucking Birthday.

I dropped them off at school saying that it would probably be me that picked them up, and made my way to work, late again.

CHAPTER 15

THE END IS NIGH

When they finished reading, Leann offered the paper back to me, but I told them they could keep it, so she tucked it into her book with the rest of her notes.

'I know it's not proof, but that's the best I've got' I said, shrugging.

Leann looked at me in a different manner. 'I don't think I need to ask you how you felt,' she said, rather tenderly.

Cooper stood up. 'Let us take a break, shall we?'

We broke for about 30 minutes. They wanted to check phone messages and touch base with the station. I also needed a break, so I walked out of the house and took a ten-minute stroll, a bit of fresh air, a mental stock take. I reviewed what I had said and not said, what had I omitted, what else there was to say. We sat back down with a new brew for everyone. I was getting tired, mentally, not physically, but I knew we had nearly finished.

So we had reached up to about three months ago. The concluding part.

CHAPTER 16

PAINTED RED

She came back after a couple of days. I understood that Kevin had mentioned to a friend that she had moved in with him, and the friend had told someone else and then the whole street and everyone in the pub knew. Someone mentioned it to her at the shops, and she went ballistic.

Meanwhile I had been to see a solicitor, a very understanding young lady who listened to my tale, took notes, clarified a few points, then suggested a course of action. She drafted a letter for me to give Kate, outlining the conditions under which she could see the children and advising her to vacate the house on a permanent basis.

We have been instructed by our client regarding recent events and, in particular, with regard to his concern about the children, Luke and Taylor. We understand that you have begun a relationship with a neighbour, Kevin, and that you have recently stated, on more than one occasion, that you are going to move out and take the children. We understand that you have also, at other times, told our party that he must leave the family home at 64 River Way so that you may stay with the children. Our claimant instructs us that he neither agrees to the children being moved out of the family home, nor to move out himself. He has serious concerns about your ability to care for the children at the present time.

We understand from him that you are, and have been for some time, drinking to excess and on a daily basis. He instructs us that you are suffering with depression and are medicated for the same. He is concerned that your excessive alcohol abuse will prevent your medication from working as it should. He instructs us that there have been, of late, a number of arguments and upsetting conversations which have taken place in front of the children. We understand that the children are showing signs of distress at what is happening and he feels this must end immediately. His view is that regardless of what is happening between the two of you, in your relationship, and the difficulties you are experiencing yourself, the children must be provided with security, stability and a calm environment. In order to achieve this he has asked us to write to you and ask that you leave 64 River Way. He will remain living in the property (which is a property owned in his sole name) with the children. He believes that if you do leave you will probably stay with Kevin, who lives just a few doors away. This being the case, he is more than happy for you to see the children on a regular basis. However, he does not agree, at the present time and whilst you are drinking to excess, to you taking the children out of the house. He instructs us that once you have obtained some help with your alcohol addiction (meaning medical assistance) and he is confident that you are able to care for the children, then he would be willing to share their care with you. We do hope that the above can be agreed and we look forward to hearing from you shortly.

The solicitor further advised me: 'If we send this and she refuses to go and causes a big fuss, then I suggest you will have no option but to force her out. That means changing locks and possibly calling the police if she is causing a commotion in front of the children. Whilst all this is going on you need to do everything you can to prevent the children being exposed to these events.'

That's not me, I couldn't do that, there had to be another way. How would my boys understand that? They had been through so much. Maybe in ten years' time they would understand how much I had been hurt, but could I face ten years of them asking why I had kicked Mummy out?

I never gave her the letter.

We sat down and talked. She didn't love Kevin; she loved me and wanted us to be a family again. She knew how the kids were feeling because her mum and dad had split up when she was the same age and she didn't want the kids to live with that experience. I listened, and listened some more. I explained that I wasn't a doormat that could just be walked upon and that it would be a long road, and she had to stop drinking. She booked an appointment with the doctor to explain about her depression and then invited me to see the therapist with her.

There was a charity function at the local pub that we had committed to attend and she wanted us to go as a family so everyone could see us together. Sure enough, she got pissed. Both Nick and Kevin were there, but she ignored them and spent most of the time talking to mutual friends. I had to get her to leave, as she was shaking badly and her hands couldn't hold her glass of wine without it spilling. The boys were bored as we had been at the pub for four hours. When we got home at about 5pm, I fed the boys, bathed them and put them to bed with a story; she was asleep on the settee.

The next day she realised she'd lost her engagement ring. We spent the next two days searching everywhere and couldn't find it, so that was an expensive charity function. The biggest issue was that she told me that during all that had happened over the last two years she had never once taken that ring off. That was meant to make me feel better, but I think I had lost the will to feel better.

We went one morning to see the therapist. She mentioned that day that she had told the therapist the truth, all of it, at the last session, which meant that for the last couple of months she had been lying to the therapist, and it was costing me fifty quid a session.

I went with an open mind and heard a lot of apologies and explanations. She didn't know what she was doing and was lost in a downward spiral of depression brought on by boredom at home and alcohol. She started a drinking diary to record her consumption, feelings and the effects; she didn't want to give up yet because she had it under control, she wanted to confront the bottle. Slowly we started working on a relationship; no sex yet, I guessed I knew that was coming. We learnt how to listen to each other, how the smallest issue could set her off, how I should tell her the next morning when things went wrong, how we should be more tactile downstairs so going to bed would not mean a confrontation and having sex. I didn't understand or necessarily agree with all the suggestions, but I tried and complied.

Nick and Kevin were still around. I saw them at the pub, at the shops, walking down the street, but we avoided any contact, and she swore that she was having no contact either.

Charles died shortly after this, but she didn't go to the funeral. She started a new job and within a few months another Christmas was nearly upon us. Her New Year's resolution was to give up drinking once and for all. We went away for Christmas this year for the first time, to a log cabin in Yorkshire with a hot tub sunk into the patio. Although it didn't snow we had long walks on the beaches of Whitby and Robin Hood Bay, ate lunch out and had dinner at home. On Boxing Day her family came over and she had a few drinks but nothing over the top. Things were looking up and when we came home on the Sunday, I was full of hope and expectation for the New Year.

But as always, things went bad. She took to the bottle the moment we got through the door to our home and wouldn't give it a rest until New Year's Day. The whole family went to lunch and she apologised to all of us, explaining that she wanted one last binge before she gave up. She promised again that this was the end of the booze.

This lasted just under three weeks before she was back on the bottle. The end was nigh.

It was a normal Sunday; I had taken the boys to football and she had worked in the morning. I got a text saying she was going to the pub for lunch and we should meet her there; she had worked so hard that she was having one glass of wine. By the time we got there the first glass was gone. She got up and got another whilst perusing the menu. Soon the second was gone and the third was started before she had eaten.

I nursed my Diet Coke, knowing that we had to do some grocery shopping and I was driving. That morning she had promised the boys a cake that she would bake but we didn't have the ingredients, yet. At 3pm I took Luke off to Sainsbury's; Kate was finishing her drink, and Taylor stayed with her.

When Luke and I got back to the house, there was no sign of her. She turned up three hours later and fell through the door. Taylor told me he had been telling

Mummy that he wanted to go home but she wouldn't listen. Luke was calling her mobile but not getting a response. I had to get the kids bathed and fed, and then the Asda man turned up with a delivery of the weekly shop and I asked her if she could help, to which I got the standard response of 'Fuck off, I have had the kids all day, can't you do anything?' etc. It was an old record and it played all evening. I didn't bother coming downstairs after I had put the boys to bed. I thought she was serious about all this and now I had been kicked in the teeth again. Only three weeks after she had apologised to me and the boys, promising a brighter future, the devil was back.

This step change turned into a larger issue the next day. We were due to see the therapist about progress and it turned into a stormy session. She said she had let everyone down on Sunday and felt really bad. I explained I was really disappointed and the therapist tried to get a reason for the relapse. It ended up with her telling both of us to fuck off, she was fed up of being wrong all the time, it wasn't her fault, she had done nothing wrong, and the kids didn't die so why should I have a go at her? Then she rushed out of the therapist's house, drove home and started on the wine.

She had given up, and so had I.

The next month was spent ignoring each other. She did what she wanted to do, went to work, came home, opened a bottle and sat watching *Come Dine With Me* while I spent the day doing the domestic chores, picking the boys up, getting their homework done, making dinner for them, buying takeaways for us, bathing the kids and then bed. When the boys were asleep, she either took herself upstairs to bed without even saying goodnight or more often slept on the settee downstairs.

That had been our lives for the past three weeks until that Monday afternoon.

And I can't do this by myself,
All of these problems, they're all in your head
And I can't be somebody else
You took something perfect and painted it red.

CHAPTER 17

ITEMS OF OMISSION

A few more questions, a few more answers, some specific, some vague. They left with the computers, reminded me not to go anywhere and apologised as the toxicology results were still not in. They talked about spending the next couple of days checking up on my story. It wasn't a story, it was an experience, but I had tuned out by then, with mental fatigue.

I saw them to the door and then sat down to think. It wasn't so much what I had told them as what I hadn't told them and how they would find out what they needed to know.

So I mentally listed what I hadn't told them.

I had not mentioned drugs very often. In the first interview I'd alluded to the fact that Kate was taking coke with Nick. I didn't think this would get him into trouble, but what I didn't mention was that I had found a wrap hidden upstairs. It was in a little plastic bag with a handwritten note, something about how you can take this and think of me, a little present for you, and I gave them a copy of the note. I knew who it was from but I didn't know when it had arrived, and she never told me about it. It wasn't there when I checked the next morning.

I wondered if she ever knew what a present that was. I had spoken about the time I had come back from holiday and thought someone had been in the house; the drawers were open, there was wine in the fridge. I didn't give them a copy of the note which expressed undying love and said she should change her brand of wine and drink the more expensive pinot that he had put in the fridge for her, and how it was a sweeter taste and reminded him of her, because that was what they had drunk the first time they had slept together. I had already given them a copy of one letter from Kevin. They didn't need this one.

I didn't mention the emails or the texts I had read

when she was asleep or out of the house. That was how I knew half of this, why I was always was one step ahead. I guess I told them as much as she told me and then left them to find a path to righteousness.

I don't know why, but I didn't mention the day my mother passed away. She had been ill in hospital on a care plan and was dying. I had spent a couple of hours with her on the Saturday and the family had arranged to get together on the Sunday for a pub lunch. It was a clear August day. I knew Mum's time was near and didn't really want the boys to see her and then have to remember her looking like a ghost of her former self, acting like a demented person, so I decided not to go to the hospital that morning.

We got to the pub a bit early and Kate followed glass of wine with glass of wine, ate little and let the consequences take hold. As everyone was leaving she wanted another drink, but I suggested she had had enough and got the car ready. On the way home she started on about how could I say she had had enough, who did I think I was. I was driving and the boys were strapped in the back playing with their DS games. She got louder and louder, wanting me to stop the car so she could get out. Then she said she hoped my mother would die and she hoped I would too. It was at this point that I remember turning to her and thinking the same, wishing she would die and leave us alone.

That evening I got a call from my sister to say my mum had passed away. Kate was asleep on the settee, and I was bathing the kids. I told her later that night and she said sorry, but I wasn't sure what she was sorry for.

That night I had a dream. I was driving down a dark country lane with the boys and she was sitting in the back between them, hitting one and then the other, right, left, right, left. The car lights picked up a sign up ahead on the road that read 'People can be cruel and they will be, People can break your heart and they will, but only you can stop them from keeping hurting you'. The reason I didn't tell Cooper or Leann is that I can't tell that story without thinking that at that time I wished she would die and leave us alone.

I didn't tell them about life before children, either. They were so focused on the recent past that they never asked what life had been like before children. I didn't volunteer much I must say, a few comments on how we met, what we did before we had children, when the boys were born, nothing more than that. If I had known then what I know now, things would have been very different, but back then I believed everything she said; I had no reason to doubt what I was being told.

We went out together and separately. I was working for an international company and was abroad some days and she was working, which required travelling and staying in hotels. We had been living in my flat for about three months when she called me late one evening, saying she was at a work function and they had gone out clubbing afterwards. I knew she was staying over at a hotel somewhere so I was surprised to get a call at 1:20 in the morning. She had lost her handbag with keys, phone and everything in it, and she was pissed as well so it was difficult to work out what was going on. I extracted the information that she had been in a club called the Red Dragon and then got a taxi, and she didn't know what to do. I asked her what room she was in and recorded the hotel phone number. Eventually I got through to the club and sure enough they had found a handbag left under a table that matched the description I gave them, so I asked them to keep it there and she would pick it up the next day.

I then phoned her back on the hotel number and was put through to her room. I had spent the last forty-five minutes finding her handbag, so I was a bit annoyed that no one answered. I tried again and this time she answered, slightly out of breath and wondering why I was calling. She had forgotten that she had lost her handbag, or even that she had called me. I explained that I had found it and she could pick it up at the club the next day after 8am. There was a lot of noise in the background, and she put her hand over the mouthpiece before coming back to me. She said she had to go as she was falling asleep, told me she loved me and put the phone down. Just one of the instances before the children when I lost her.

After we had been together for nearly a year I suggested we should get engaged and bought her a beautiful ring. Although she was always known as Mrs Donaldson, we never got round to getting married, although we did manage to get pregnant.

I didn't tell the officers about the time when Luke was three months old and I was working and had to attend a corporate black tie dinner. She found a baby sitter and went out with a female friend, saying she was going for a drink with her after she had finished work, just for an hour or two. As I was half way through my dinner, discussing next month's budgets and forcast with my senior management, I got an emergency call saying she was lost, couldn't get home and I had to get home as soon as possible as the babysitter had to leave. She could hardly speak, her words distorted and incomprehensible through the fog of alcohol. I made my apologiers, left the dinner and drove back home, picked up the little one and put him in the car. I then dropped the babysitter home and went driving around looking for Kate. She had turned her phone off and I had no idea where she was, but I was guessing she was in a local pub.

All of a sudden I got a text to say she was outside a park in Chertsey, just a few miles away. I found her sitting on a park bench, her clothes muddy, her jeans torn at the knees and her eyes glazed over. She fell into the car and mumbled 'Don't ask, just get me home'. I drove home, put Luke to bed and found her passed out on the settee. The next morning she explained she had gone for a drink withthese two guys from her firnds work and then she remembered nothing, except that she fell over in a park. She didn't know how her jeans had got so muddy or torn. She thought the guys might have spiked her drink, but she wouldn't recognise them if she saw them again so there was no point in reporting it to anyone. She didn't know what pub she had been to ; her friend had left her talking to these guys at the bar as she had to get home, she remembered her firend leaving. She said she had had it with drinking, this wouldn't happen again and told me how much she loved me.

I wasn't the type to be checking up on her then. I wished I had, as a lot of this would have been avoided and I wouldn't have been sitting there feeling guilty after all I had been put through.

CHAPTER 18

WHAT'S MISSING?

Cooper started the car and sat there for a while before pulling away.

'Well you were right, Saga Part 2 was as bad as Saga Part 1,' he said finally.

Leann smiled. 'This is a right old mess. The more he talked, the more I felt sorry for him. I think I was expecting a short conclusion rather than another session of woe.'

Cooper started listing the evidence as they drove.

'The good thing is that dates and people are defined, so that helps. He kept sporadic diaries to remind him of the bad times, which is a bit weird, but I guess if they were going to split up it would be good evidence in court to win custody of the children. I am assuming here that he would want custody?'

'There's no way she would have got custody, not if he can prove any of these stories.'

'So checking all this should be easy. We need to work out a motive. If it's not suicide it could be him, or one of the two guys mentioned. Does he seem cold enough not just to harm her but to kill her?'

Leann pondered this. 'If anyone did kill her then I think it is possible that he did.'

'Based on what?'

'Based on his lack of emotion. He's very logical, factual... I don't know.'

'But why now?'

'I don't know, I'm thinking out loud... so they have spent the last three weeks living in the house with her suggestion that they do their own thing, which he obviously is not comfortable with, but what happened in the last three weeks that made a shift? We need to focus on the last three weeks, find out where they went separately, who contacted them, what they have been up to.'

'But he's already told us they have not done

anything recently.'

'Do you believe him?'

'Well he's been pretty up front up to now, he's told us stuff we didn't need to hear. Do you not?'

'I believe his version but I don't know hers, no one will. Maybe the therapist will help. When are you seeing her?'

'Tomorrow's Thursday, right?'

'Yes.'

'Tomorrow at 9:30am, and you're seeing the two guys? Are you taking someone with you?'

'Naturally, procedure demands it.'

'Yes I know, but I also know what you are like with procedure.'

Leann smiled. 'I'm taking Mary Abbott, if that's OK with you sir.'

'Good choice, although you two together are as thick as thieves sometimes.'

'Do you think we're missing something, sir?'

Cooper responded immediately. 'We are missing plenty, motive and opportunity. We're already thinking of this as a murder case when we don't know the results yet but if we don't move now then we might be too late to investigate, if it is murder. As for your question, I think we are missing something big. If it's murder, why now?'

CHAPTER 19

LINES OF NORMALITY

The alarm clock above my head showed just after two in the morning. I lay awake, Luke's head resting on my left arm and Taylor buried in my right armpit, all three of us tangled up in the king-size bed. During brighter times the four of us had frequently shared the bed, both little ones cuddled next to me, but that was never going to happen again.

The house was quiet. My mother-in-law was asleep in the spare room, dealing with her grief in her own way. We had agreed not to talk about what had happened, for the time being. She knew her daughter was a bit of a rebel, and she knew we had been having difficulties. I had phoned her several times over the past years asking her to talk to Kate, but all she got was half-truths and lies. My mother-in-law was as helpless as I was to deal with this.

I extrapolated myself from the various arms and legs that had me pinned down and kissed my boys as they slept, promising that I would always put them first. Then I crept downstairs. When the bad times were upon us I used to do this frequently, come downstairs in the middle of the night, get a drink, sometimes have a smoke. I would check that the oven hadn't been left on and turn the TV and lights off, as they had invariably been left on. I was used to not making a sound, and I knew each stair that creaked; I didn't want to wake her.

But tonight, as for the rest of my life, I wouldn't be able to wake her. She had gone forever. There was no mess, no empty wine bottles left sprawled around the room for me to tidy up, nothing for me to be concerned about.

I got myself a drink of milk and sat down on the settee. The questions still reverberated around my head. Could I have done something different? Was everything my fault? How would I cope? What would normal look like now?

After each step change there would be a period of calm, when I would try and talk to her. I used to explain that there was a line of normality, a set of rules, or rather guidelines, that you needed to live by to make a relationship work. Each step change moved that line of normality down and it was very difficult to bring it back up. A guideline suggesting that going to the pub at lunchtime on your own is not an issue, so that guideline is adhered to. The line of normality drops when the trip to the pub becomes every day. Obviously this is not a single step change but more of a gradual decline, until you realise that this line has become the new normal. The line drops again when it becomes an evening drink for an hour which soon turns into three or four hours. Getting back from the pub at closing time may be acceptable, but if the norm becomes two hours after closing time it has shifted again. Going round to Kevin's for a quick drink to discuss Charles's care soon turned into getting back at 2am and then went on to staying the night. When that becomes the norm, there is something seriously wrong.

That line of normality drives behaviour, action and reaction. Could I have reacted differently? What would have been the outcome, what would have changed? Standing at the door shouting for her not to go out with the boys standing next to me was not enough. Could I have done more? There might have been a week or a month during which she hadn't told me to fuck off and die. I was elated, bur looking back, why should I be elated at that?

I looked around the room, the photos on the walls, mostly of her and the two boys, smiling and laughing. There wasn't one of me, I guess because I had the camera. Would it have been too much to ask her to take a photograph of me and the boys, just once? I realised that I hadn't asked for anything; if I wanted something then I would do it myself. I remembered times during her delusional behaviour when it seemed she would spend the evening asking me to do everything. She would walk from the kitchen to the lounge, sit down and then ask me to close the kitchen door, a silly thing to ask. Why didn't she do it, why ask me? Was it all to do with being in control, or was it something more? As I had got used to these commands I had just got up and closed the door. I recalled the time when I wanted to have a shower and told her I was going upstairs, and she asked me not to dirty the towels as she had just washed them. So how was I supposed to dry myself?

There were lots of these incidents. I complied as best as I could, without argument, but I realised recently that I had lost who I was. That's why I had looked for solutions, and could only come up with one.

I closed my eyes, tried to picture Luke, Taylor and me running along a beach, jumping the waves, playing football in the sand, but whatever pictures came into my mind there was a ghostly shadow watching from the periphery.

CHAPTER 20

OPPORTUNITY AND MOTIVE

At the police station, Cooper and Leann entered the room they had booked for the afternoon, coffee in one hand, papers and computers stuck under their arms. The room was empty apart from a desk, a couple of chairs and two large whiteboards on adjacent walls. They put down their stuff on the desk and pulled out the chairs. It was just after lunch and they were planning to be here for at least 8 hours.

Cooper started. 'I hope you have cancelled your

social life tonight, because we're going to get to the bottom of this today. I plan on going to see him tomorrow after we have seen the CPS.'

'Yes I have.' Leann was trying her hardest not to call him sir.

'I told the wife to entertain herself tonight as she should be in bed before I get home, however if we get done in time I might just buy you a drink on the way home.'

'I might just accept.'

'OK, let's get started.'

Leann stood up with some of the whiteboard markers in her hand. She approached the board on the left and wrote at the top three words: Opportunity, Motive and How. Underneath she drew horizontal lines, roughly equidistant, where they would put their notes. 'Let's leave out the husband, just for now?' she suggested. She then went to the other board and down the left-hand side possible suspects - Nick, Kevin, other, none - in rows and drew identical horizontal lines.

She looked at Cooper. 'Have I missed anything?'

'You didn't put the priest up there.'

She turned and went to write before it dawned on her that Cooper's sense of humour sometimes got the better of her.

'OK, what have we got to start with?'

After the first debrief they had divided the list. Cooper got the therapist, as he thought she was the key. Leann had got both Nick and Kevin as they both felt, knowing what they did, that a woman's touch would be useful. For the rest of the list they had sent a few plods to do the groundwork and if they came up with anything interesting then either Cooper or Leann would follow up. This morning they had interviewed all the officers who had worked the case. They had received a report from the computer department regarding Joseph Donaldson's computer, they had had a preliminary report from toxicology and pathology and they had also had a return call from the priest, who had enthusiastically offered to come in, but they decided that wasn't needed, just a few background checks.

With all the notes collated, they decided to lock themselves away for the afternoon. They had a history of working on cases and found that just the two of them, with some blue sky thinking and a couple of whiteboards, worked best for them. They had to come up with something that night, as the CPS officer that there were seeing in the morning doesn't like being messed around.

The objective was threefold: firstly, decide if one or more persons were responsible for a loss of life, secondly, what was the motive behind the action or actions, not only why but what or who would gain from it, and thirdly how it had been done, Cooper was mindful of the other missing piece - why now?

They decided to concentrate on three people, Joe Donaldson, Nick and Kevin. There was one other possible outcome; they crossed out 'other' on the board and put 'suicide.' Each outcome was to be given a timeslot and a conclusion had to be reached by that time.

But first they had to address a general issue; what had killed her. Both Cooper and Leann had met with the pathologist that morning. Brenda White was only 24 but well respected within the police community. Most people thought she lived for her work, and she never joined the ranks for after-work drinks or even Christmas parties. She was fluent in medical mumbo jumbo and several times they both had to interrupt her so they could understand not only the facts and the idiosyncrasies but also the nuisances of the toxicology report. 'Although commonly misinterpreted, pathology and toxicology are not an exact science' she said several times, much to Cooper and Leann's hidden amusement. If they weren't exact sciences, what was?

However the outcome and the concluding summary did not bode well for Cooper and Leann.

'We are still in preliminary status and we're still progressing tests, but if we don't know what we're looking for then we can't find it,' said Leann. 'However, as of this moment I can confirm three things: you will need to take these things and decide what to do with them, as that is not my job. I am not here to provide conjecture, offer opinion or even apportion blame. My job is to tell you the facts, the whole facts and nothing but the facts.'

'OK. As I said earlier, there are three issues that you need to deal with. Firstly she had taken cocaine that day, as you suggested, however the preliminary test shows that the substance may have been contaminated, and no, I cannot say deliberately, I don't know. If I was asked in court, I would have to testify no. Outside of court I would say deliberately. I have seen this before come up in tests. Crushing rat or ant poison into the coke will not be visible or affect the taste but it can be lethal. I tested for a chemical called deltamethrin, common in such poisons, but on its own it is not lethal. However, before you jump out of your seats, let me take you to the second anomaly. It appears that her blood and liver showed considerable amounts of recent and long-term alcohol abuse, and I mean abuse. This you also already know, but what you didn't know was that I found some decontamination as well. In her stomach, implying recent intake, there were traces of sodium hypochlorite, a main ingredient of household bleach - don't ask me what make or type.

Again there is no way I could testify in court that the wine was deliberately infused with household bleach, but outside court I would say that it was very possible. Now bleach would be detectable on the palate if sufficient amounts were placed in a glass, but in a bottle and stirred, and then drunk by someone whose palate had already been infected, and who is a bit high on coke - well you can deduce the rest, I hope.'

Cooper bravely interrupted. 'So both substances could or could not have been deliberately or unintentionally contaminated, by one or more people per substance, which could or could not have caused enough harm to kill, with or without intention.' The sentence had started off with anticipation, but had faded into despair as the realisation was filling in. 'We also cannot tell if one or both substances were consumed deliberately or knowingly'

Brenda smiled. 'I think what you said was correct. There are none of the forced consumption marks that we would have expected, so we can all agree that what she took she took of her own accord.'

'And the third thing?' Leann asked.

'As I don't give opinions, all I can say is that the amount of contamination would not normally have caused death, but the delay in hospitalisation and the apparent unwillingness of the patient to fight the effects by not vomiting seem to be contributing factors.'

'You mean she might have just given up?'

Brenda nodded. 'It happens.'

This effectively concluded Brenda's input, and she left with the standard, 'If there is anything else you want, or if you find a specific substance you want me to test for, I am just down the corridor, you know where to find me. Sorry I couldn't have been more specific.'

Leann and Cooper thanked her for her input, both unsure whether there was anything she had said that could add light to the investigation. Cooper suggested starting with his interview findings. He had opted to go and see Kaz the therapist by himself whilst Leann had concentrated on Nick and Kevin.

'Let me tell you what happened with Kaz, then you tell me about Nick and Kevin' he said. 'I had a very interesting couple of hours with her, but I'm not sure what I got out of it.'

CHAPTER 21

KAZ

Detective Inspector Cooper drove up the avenue searching for number 54. It turned out to be a three-bedroom terraced house at the back of a clean and tidy estate, probably built in the 1970s. He parked up and locked his car, opened the garden gate and strode up a short path bisecting a well-maintained lawn to reach the door. He had spoken to Kaz the day before and had been lucky to get a slot in her diary for 10 am. He wasn't too surprised to see the door open before he had managed to ring the bell; he guessed that she would be as apprehensive as he was. Although he had met several counsellors during his professional years he had never had the opportunity to interview one in their own surroundings. He felt a bit nervous, which he knew was stupid, and he couldn't help thinking how her patients must feel coming up this path for the first time, about to bare their souls and tell their secrets to a stranger.

A woman was standing at the door wearing slightly baggy jeans, a plain blouse and a cardigan with a flower scarf around her neck. She had long nearly-black hair, tied up behind her head, and extended her long fingered hand to welcome the detective. The word 'bohemian' came to mind.

'Detective Inspector Cooper, I assume' she said with a slight smile.

Cooper assessed her. She was about 50 with a slightly pointed face. Her smile and demeanour were warm and friendly.

'Please call me James,' he said.

'Fine James, please come in and take a seat.'

She extended her arm towards a front room and a settee placed in front of the bay window. James entered and sat down, noticing a glass of water had been placed ready for him on a small table next to the settee. Kaz closed the door behind her, sat opposite and leaned forward.

'I am sorry,' she began. 'Normally my profession requires me to listen and not talk, so if I am a bit nervous...'

'That's fine Kaz. Firstly, thank you for seeing me so promptly and for your hospitality. Secondly you have an unusual name. Kaz - is it short for anything?'

'Oh.' She blushed slightly. 'I was named after Katharine Hepburn, I think my parents wanted me to be a missionary.'

'Like in *African Queen*?'

'Exactly, but I got fed up with people spelling my name wrong.'

'That's right, it is spelt with an "a", not an "e".'

'You know your movies James. I didn't like Kat and ended up with Kaz.'

'Hollywood has always been a side interest of mine.'

They both took a drink. Cooper went into professional mode.

'As you are aware from our telephone conversation, I am here to discuss a patient of yours whom we found dead on Monday, Kate Donaldson. Mr Donaldson gave us your name. I understand you knew them both, and he suggested we speak to you. Currently we do not know the cause of death as we're waiting for toxicology results, but our first impression is that Mrs Donaldson either killed herself or was poisoned via alcohol or drugs.' He took a sip of water. 'I would like to ask a few questions, but I think it would be more productive if you just tell me what you can. I am trying to get a picture of them both. There seem to be a lot of conflicting stories, initially I would like to corroborate what Mr Donaldson has said on his statement, if that's OK with you?'

He took her silence as agreement.

'So tell me from the start, probably your first meeting? I will try not to interrupt too much.'

'Well, firstly I was shocked to hear the news, but looking back I wasn't exactly surprised. In my time counselling I see a lot of people and some are troubled to the extent where you don't know if you are getting through to them at all, or even if they want you to. I understand Mrs Donaldson got my name from the internet. She told me when we first met that she was having trouble coping with living at home and was turning to alcohol too much. I remember our first meeting; she was very nervous and mentioned that her husband had suggested she saw a counsellor as things were getting out of hand. She explained that she had two children and was struggling to cope, either with the boredom now their kids were at school and the chaos when they were home. She said her husband was a good man who would do anything for the kids and she was worried that she couldn't match him for their affections or time, and that drove her to drink.

'In the first couple of meetings it emerged that she was drinking every day, but the problem was that once or twice a week she would take this to a different level and consume maybe three bottles of wine in the day. She had started drinking before lunchtime as part of her work commitment to help an elderly man. She had begun having a social drink with him and another man, Kevin, before lunch; she would then pick the kids up and take them home, sometimes by car, and in the evenings when the husband returned she would go back round to this elderly guy's house and end up drinking there with Kevin or going round to Kevin's house.

'She explained that her husband wasn't happy at all as she was neglecting the children and him and spending more and more time round at Kevin's. She explained that Kevin understood her as he liked drinking and he was very good at listening. I remember she mentioned that Kevin knew things about her that her husband didn't.' She stopped and took a drink of water, then continued.

'She also mentioned that her husband couldn't understand why she was going out and several times he suggested that maybe she was having an affair. So he did not trust her, and this made her go out more.

'I suggested that she should keep a drinking diary and she duly obliged, and turned up to each meeting with a record of alcohol consumption, but she rarely filled in the sections asking why, and how she felt afterwards. She wasn't stupid, she knew what she was doing was ruining her life at home, but she didn't seem to care. However as she was coming to see me, that became a dilemma that I couldn't fathom. Why was she coming if she didn't care?

'I met them both after four sessions. I invited Mr Donaldson to come and share his thoughts. It was an interesting meeting. She was very much the dominant one and she hardly let him speak, but he acknowledged that he was jealous of her going out and was worried about her drinking.

'She told me about an affair she had had a few years before and explained what had happened and how they had tried to put it behind them, but what was interesting was what happened when I met them both and asked him about it. His view was that it wasn't an issue any more. It had happened and she had sworn on the children's lives that it wouldn't happen again. However he talked about the fallout of the pregnancy and the abortion, which was news to me. I had spent four weeks with her and she hadn't told me that she had got pregnant or had an abortion by another man. Why not?'

Kaz stopped for another drink. 'Do you know about this? I am assuming I am filling in blanks to a story you already know the main details to.'

Cooper sat back, nodding. 'That's correct. I have a very long story from the husband and at the moment you are kindly supporting the main parts, which makes my life a lot easier. Please go on.'

'Our sessions continued on a bi-weekly basis, sometimes here, sometimes at their house, but when I went there she often had a glass of wine in her hand when I arrived. She thought it would help me if I saw her drinking, I'm not sure why. Then we had another problem. I got a call from her about three months into our sessions. She was drunk and slurring her speech. She wanted to see me as soon as possible and we arranged to meet the next day. She was in a state when she arrived and looked like she hadn't slept for a couple of days. She sat down and started telling me the truth about Kevin. She had been having an affair with him for five months. She had lied to me, her husband and the children. She said she had finally told them the truth and was moving out to live with Kevin. She also said that she had gone back to seeing the man she had got pregnant with, if I remember right his name was Nick, and she had dug herself into such a hole that she wanted to kill herself.'

Cooper nodded again, to indicate that they knew most of this.

'I kept in touch with her nearly daily, for a week,

and it all changed again - she didn't want Kevin, he had told someone she was moving in with him and how happy he was, although she was furious that he had told anyone, and now she wanted her life back with her husband and kids. This was a complete turnaround. To be honest I had no idea what she was thinking, she was very mixed up. Is this useful?'

'Yes, please go on.'

'So I hosted a meeting between her and her husband where she pleaded guilty to everything and said nothing would happen again, she would give up drinking and she wanted everything to be back to normal. As a professional I had to drive to what were the key issues that needed to be addressed. The husband was surprisingly positive and explained that the three things that needed to be addressed were communication, affection and alcohol. I understood they had not had sex for six months, to which she explained that she couldn't until she felt that their relationship was back on track.

'The husband wasn't as animated as I thought he would be. He was quiet and resigned. He knew what he wanted but he didn't know how to get there. I had a few meetings with him on his own and found him charming, if reserved, but there was something about him that I couldn't put my finger on. Only once in all the sessions did he get angry. He explained in no uncertain words that he was the victim, she had ruined everything and she was making out that it wasn't her fault. This became an ongoing issue, as I believe that she really thought everyone else was to blame. That highlighted her paranoia. It seemed to get worse when she drank, but basically I had diagnosed her as showing symptoms of a schizophrenic paranoid alcoholic. This is the most common form of schizophrenia. It's basically a subtype of schizophrenia where the patient has delusions and false beliefs that people are always plotting against them. In a mild form it can manifest as not believing anything that anybody is saying about them, so if the husband said that she was drunk and really argumentative she would believe that he had made it up just to make her feel bad. It is also associated with delusions of grandeur, where the patient believes they are untouchable, in a greater-than-thou way, or even physically more powerful, which might be reflected in the physical attacks on the husband. This particular subtype does not generally affect concentration, memory or emotions, which allows the a patient to function almost normally. It is a known complication that can lead to deeper complications, including suicide, but more readily anger, aggression, condescension and detachment, all of which have been shown over the past sessions.

'Now add that concoction to an alcohol dependency and you have a volatile cocktail of personality change and disorders. It is well known that most paranoid schizophrenics suffer from substance abuse, depression and tobacco addiction. As you paint your picture you will see that all these are visible in this case.

'Saying all that, I think I could see the husband's views. Underneath there was somebody inside who knew what she was doing, wanted to stop but couldn't be bothered to put the effort in, does this make sense?'

'Yes it does, this is very interesting,' said Cooper. 'Just a quick question, why didn't her doctor see this?'

'Let's just take this case rather than a generic diagnosis. I believe, and I am sure you can check with her doctor, that she didn't tell the doctor the whole of the issue. She probably mentioned tiredness, and maybe alcoholic dependency, even depression but when explained in individual terms it is difficult to make a sum of the whole. With me, although she didn't tell me everything to begin with, the more time we spent together the more I saw her unravel and therefore the easier it was to diagnose. I think she deliberately didn't tell me everything, and if you think about the delusions of grandeur that I mentioned earlier this would be a classic symptom, cause and effect.'

'Ok, I'll speak to the doctor, please continue.'

'Well we, all three of us, spent the next couple of months trying to put some effort into the relationship, which had some success. They would turn up and say they had had a good couple of weeks and both showed how they had made effort and also identified areas where they could work better. She was still drinking but she had put a date in the diary to give up, maybe forever. We still had the odd episode when she would go on a binge and undo all the good work, but as the husband pointed out, there were no consequences or compunction.'

Cooper lifted an eyebrow at 'compunction'. He had heard the word only at church, a long time ago.

'I mean, she would say sorry but then go and do it again. Sorry wasn't sorry, it was some sort of "OK, you got me". As we approached the New Year she was supposed to giving up drinking and arranged to see me on her own. I think New Year was on a Thursday and she came on the Monday and the first day that she had been dry was the Sunday, she hadn't wanted to start on New Year's Day. Anyway she explained that they had been away for Christmas and all had been well, and she was looking forward to a new beginning.

'However at our next session the three of us met up; it was the 17th January, I know as it was the last session we had. The husband was quiet and she explained that she had gone out on the Sunday and got drunk again, but didn't remember arguing. When I approached the husband for his thoughts he told a story about her hitting him just before the New Year when she had been drinking all day. I was amazed that after all our time in sessions she had started leaving out significant incidents. The husband mentioned again that he was fed up with all the broken promises and if she didn't want to put any effort into building a relationship she should move out. This made her flip – she started swearing and shouting and stormed out. That was a new one for me. He stayed and talked about things he wanted. To me he just wanted a normal relationship and what they were in now wasn't a relationship. I wished him well and hoped I would see them again, however something inside told me I wouldn't.'

Kaz stopped talking and took another sip of water. 'That's about it, I guess.'

'Thank you very much, that was very interesting. Can I ask you a few questions and then get a professional opinion?'

'Of course.'

'Firstly, who paid for these sessions? I guess you're not cheap.' Cooper smiled.

'He did, paid by cheque. She kept a log of how much and when to pay and he wrote cheques. Any reason for the question?'

'Not to appear critical of your professional ability, but to me he wasted a lot of his money on her, especially if things weren't going well. I understand that her not telling you the truth put you in a difficult situation.'

'Yes, it was difficult. To be honest he was very optimistic that she would wake up one day and see the light. He believed that deep down she could understand, but the other side of her personality grew darker. He told me that with every episode it couldn't get darker. He felt that they had hit the bottom of the well several times, but every time they started making their way up the well became deeper, the walls steeper. So right to the end he was hoping upon hope.'

'Secondly, based on your professional assessment, could she take her own life?'

'Yes definitely, although normally people threaten suicide to get attention. The suicide rate is higher in people who don't mention that they might kill themselves.'

'OK, I get that. Could the husband have killed her?'

'That's a tough one. My initial reaction is no, he's been through the mill for sure, but where or what would the motive be, financial?'

'That's what we're missing, what would be the motive now.'

They sat in silence for a few moments.

'Lastly, what can you tell me about these other guys, Nick and Kevin?' asked Cooper.

'Well you first must accept that she didn't tell me the truth on a lot of levels and I believe that she really didn't know what she felt about either one of them. Let me think.' She paused for a moment. 'Nick, I believe, was a one off that then turned into something else, like an escape from her normal life. I don't think she thought that much of him, but she may have given him a different impression. As the relationship went on I think by what she was saying was that he wanted more. I wasn't sure when or how this one finished but I believe he was being kept on a string, just in case. She mentioned that he continued to call her and hoped she would come back soon.

'Kevin on the other hand was a different proposition, a wealthy older man with a lot of time on his hands. I think he really fell for her and I believe she saw him as a way out but in a more permanent sense. She spent a lot of time with him just sitting and talking. She mentioned once that Kevin knew everything about her, which implies that she told Kevin about Nick. My guess is that Kevin also saw this as a last chance to find someone to live with him and he fell deeply for her. I am not sure how Nick would have responded when he found out about Kevin; I think he might have been quite angry.

'As for Kevin, when they split up she mentioned several times that he approached her by letter, making phone calls and trying to bump into her in the street. She had ignored all attempts, or so she told me. The fallout between the two could have had quite serious consequences, but I'm only going on my opinion of people I never met. Although thinking about it, during the last few individual sessions we had she did think that she was being followed or watched. I'm not sure if that was just paranoia.'

'Do you know if either of them had access to the house?'

'I'm pretty sure she mentioned that Kevin had a key. I remember something about coming home from holiday and her husband noticing some things had changed. She dismissed them as rubbish, but she never told me whether she suspected anything. As for Nick, I don't know, I'm afraid.'

Cooper stood up. 'Thanks again for your time and hospitality. I'll leave you my number. If you think of anything else you can call me anytime.'

Kaz took the offered business card and placed it on the table. They shook hands and she saw Cooper to the door.

CHAPTER 22

WHERE'S NICK?

Leann had taken WPC Mary Abbott with her. They had been friends for a few years; they were both single and lived not far from each other. They had met by accident when they were both called to a domestic dispute just doors away from the road they both lived on. Leann not only enjoyed Mary's company but respected her point of view, particularly when it came to assessing people. She was slim and no taller than Leann, but she was also a black belt in Judo and could handle herself; as they didn't quite know what they were going to encounter, Leann wasn't taking chances. They had both donned their uniforms earlier to portray an immediate air of authority. Mary had a way of saying it as it was, and they often shared an inappropriate joke, usually to the detriment of one of the male officers. They also shared a similarly eclectic taste in music.

All they had to go on was the pub name and Nick's first name. The landlady of the Dog and Partridge and Pigeon was Rebecca, a real northern lass and a stereotypical landlady, with lots of smiles and very welcoming. They had rung earlier and she was waiting for them as they walked through the door, wearing a red shift dress that showed a little too much cleavage. If you were polite you would call her plump, or less politely, rotund.

The few locals who were sitting at the bar turned quickly as the women walked in. The place went quiet as Rebecca ushered them through to the back room. A small space which was obviously a restaurant area was separated from the lounge by an open arch at the end of the main bar.

Leann introduced herself and Mary and took out her pocket book to write notes if necessary. 'Thanks for seeing us, not very busy? She asked'

'Not yet' replied Rebecca. 'The workers are outside

in the smoking shed and the darts team get here about six, so it's a normal early evening crowd.'

'You know why we are here. We're looking for a guy called Nick. We don't know much else, but we have reason to believe he had an affair with the lady who was found dead earlier in the week.'

'Yes, I heard about that. She was a regular in here. I've known her husband and the family for years, please send them my personal condolences. We've had a whip round and sent a card and flowers.'

'We would really like to talk to you about your take on this, and we would like to find this guy called Nick. Did you know about the affair?'

'Not a lot gets past me. At first she just came in and hung around with the guys. They would buy her drinks, but when she came in with her husband most of them ignored her. I then started noticing that Nick would slip away from the crowd and buy just two drinks, one for her and one for him, and they would go out for a smoke together. At closing time they would leave together. At the time we thought it was an honourable thing and he was just walking her home. You have to understand she was often consuming two bottles of wine at least, and when she arrived she looked like she had had a few before she had even got here. Many a time she was unstable on her feet.'

Rebecca then remembered her responsibilities as

landlady. 'I did ban her a few times and I also put a drink restriction on her, but I could not legislate for what she had drunk before she came in,' she quickly added. 'Then there was the odd night when Nick didn't come in, which was unusual, and no one knew where he had gone - he didn't answer his phone when the guys called him. He would brush it off the next night as the guys ribbed him about stashing away a mystery woman. I put two and two together when I saw them meeting outside the pub one night, and instead of coming in they walked down the road towards Nick's house. I think a couple of the guys guessed, or he told them. He was very pleased with himself, as she was very attractive and way out of his league. It must have gone on for a while, but it seemed to stop and start, it was if they didn't see each other for a month and then it would be back on again. I should have told the husband, but I had no real proof. Then it all stopped for good, I don't know why, and she stopped coming in. Nick still came in but over the next few months he was getting really drunk and becoming aggressive, so I banned him to for a couple of weeks. After that he seemed to lose a bit of himself. Am I talking too much?'

'Not at all,' encouraged Leann. 'You're being very helpful.'

'Then we had another issue when she came in with another man called Kevin, one of her close neighbours.

This caused a bigger stir, although they only came in at lunchtime. Over the next few months he looked like the cat that had got the cream, but then disappeared and hasn't been in since. The rumour in the bar was that she was leaving her husband and kids and going to live with Kevin. Do you know all this?'

'Most of it but, thanks for corroborating some aspects. Just a few quick questions. Off the record, what do you know about drugs in the pub?'

'I run a tight ship here, it's a traditional pub and no drugs come through the door. However I am aware that Nick had access to some substances, mainly Charlie, sorry cocaine. I could tell when he had been on it, and that was one of the reasons he was banned, you could tell.'

'OK, thank you. Do you know where Nick is now or where he lives? Do you know his surname?'

'I know all three. His surname is Martin, and he lives two roads down, Penton Avenue, Flat Number 12. As for where he is now, you just walked past him. He's the bald one in the smoking shed outside. If you wait five minutes it's his round next so he'll be in. If you stay here I'll send him over, once he's paid for the drinks. By the way, can I get you anything?

'No thanks', Mary and Leann replied together.

'Ok, I'll send him over.'

CHAPTER 23

OUT WITH NICK

Leann got up and stretched her legs as Mary sat re-reading the notes that Leann had provided, a summary of the interview she and Cooper had carried out the day before. She looked at the picture of Kate and Joseph Donaldson that Leann had borrowed. They looked happy on a sunny beach, and she was smiling and looking into his eyes.

'She was attractive,' said Mary.

'Yep, they made a lovely couple, on the outside,' Leann replied.

Just then a man walked through the arch rather apprehensively with a pint in one hand, and Mary slipped the photograph behind her notebook. He was trying to look confident as he strode towards them and held out his hand. He was about 50 years old, with a builder's physique, a shaven head, a very prominent nose and a few large tattoos showing on his thick arms under his T-shirt.

'Er hi, er Rebecca said you would like to talk to me? I'm Nick.'

Leann and Mary shook the calloused hand. The officers introduced themselves and Leann motioned for Nick to sit down. Leann glanced at Mary; this wasn't what they had been expecting. In the car on the way down they had speculated about what sort of person this Nick would be and decided he would be a slightly older man, quite good-looking with a distinctive charm. They had been wrong on that score.

'Nick Martin, yes? Address 12 Penton Avenue?'

'That's me. How can I help?'

Leann looked straight into his eyes and saw fear. From the way his eyes were darting around the room nervously, she suspected he had had a rough night last night. Although this was probably his second drink, he didn't look good on it.

'Firstly, thanks for your time,' she said. 'I am assuming you have only had one drink as I would like you to be sober when we talk to you.'

'Yeah sure, just finished work about an hour ago, it started raining so we downed tools. I work for myself so I can clock off anytime I like. I met the guys about 30 minutes ago.' he took a sip from his pint.

'It's about the lady up the road who died on Monday, I guess you heard about it?'

'Er yeah, I heard, nice lady.'

Mary decided to help Leann out. 'We have reason to believe that you knew this lady and that you were involved with her. Can you confirm this?'

'Er yeah, I know her - knew her - and yeah, we did have something going on but not for the last six months.'

'Was it you who broke it off?'

'Er no, not really, in fact I tried calling her and asking her why she broke it off, we had a real good thing going, you know.'

'You did know she was married and had two children?' Mary asked with a touch of sarcasm.

'Yeah, but she really liked me, said she was going to leave him. Everyone has affairs.' He grinned at Mary though crooked teeth as some confidence came into his demeanour.

Mary bent her head and started taking notes, so Leann took over.

'When did you meet and how did this all start? Please tell us in your own words.'

Nick leaned back in his chair, took a couple of gulps of his pint and began.

'She and her husband used to come in about once a month, I think they had a baby sitter. They would sit quietly in the corner. They knew a couple of guys that I knew. She used to drink, I mean really drink, and her husband would end up taking her home. I saw her several times stagger out of the toilet, she could hardly stand. I asked around discreetly… she is – was – beautiful, everything that I would look for in a woman. The rumour was that she would come in lunchtimes as well, so for a couple of weeks I clocked myself off and came in here at lunchtimes, just in case, you know? She would be there on her own and as the pub wasn't busy we got talking. I ended up buying her drinks and walking with her to pick the kids up from school, although she wouldn't let me meet them. I asked if she ever got out in the evening and she said she was out the following week with a couple of friends, so I gatecrashed that party, bought her a few drinks more than she should have and instead of going home persuaded her to come to my flat.'

'What would you have to offer that she wanted to go to your flat? And by the way we know about the drugs, but we're not interested in that at the moment. We're focusing on the victim.'

Nick hesitated and then continued.

'She had mentioned that she used to take coke before she had children, and that's what I offered - come over to my place you can smoke, drink and take coke. It was like taking a baby to a sweet shop. So we ended up in bed and she left about 2 am, don't know what she told her old man.' His lip lifted with a smirk of triumph.

'Then she disappeared for a while, I have no idea why, probably had a guilt complex or something. I didn't do anything as I knew she had had a good time. About three months later she was back - she and a few friends entered the pub. I was with my mates but as soon as she looked over I knew she was hooked. She sank a few bottles of wine, her friends left and she came over and sat with me, just before closing time, and we ended back at my place again. This became a regular occurrence. She told me that she hated her life, her husband beat her, her brats drove her crazy and what she wanted to do was get out of her head. Why not, you only live once. I think she wanted the coke more than me but I fell for her and would give her anything she wanted.

'Then it all went tits up again, I don't know why. I don't know if the husband found out but she disappeared, didn't come to the pub. Rumour was she had given up drinking for a while, but then the guys started saying they had seen her with an old guy called

Kevin who lives down their street. I wasn't very happy I admit. I thought we were great together, I thought she would leave and come and live with me, didn't happen. Then she winds up dead. Funny, I haven't seen Kevin around for the last three months either.'

By this time Nick had nearly finished his pint and was wondering if it would be OK to order another.

'Thank you for being honest about the drugs' Leann said. 'Did you send her letters?'

'Yeah, I did, can't remember how many, one or two. She had asked me to send her some coke so after she disappeared I sent a few letters and some coke, for personal use only.' He added the last bit quickly, still not one hundred percent certain that they wouldn't revert to the drug issues later.

'Have you had any contaminated coke?'

'No, I won't tell you where I get it but I have never had anything like that. Why do you ask?'

'Not your problem, just ticking the boxes. So you got together, split up, got back together then split up again and then found out she was sleeping this Kevin when she could have been spending her time with you. How angry were you?'

'I didn't care any more. I had tried my hardest to get her to live with me. I did go on a bender for a while but that's life. Her loss.'

Mary's face was like stone, but she was thinking

that Nick was certainly no loss. In fact she had already decided she didn't like him at all. She turned towards him.

'How much damage do you think you did to her and her family with your little affair?'

'If it weren't me it would have been someone else. She was unhappy, that's why she went for the coke, I just had some fun that's all,' Nick replied defensively.

'That's not what you said earlier, you said that you fell for her and wanted her back. What would you do to get her back? What would you do to make sure that she wasn't with anyone else but you?'

'I got loads of girls. I didn't need her, she needed me. Now can I go and get another drink please?'

Mary threw a question in. 'Who knew about you?'

'Nobody, just between me and her.'

'What about your mate? The one you had that explosive threesome with?'

Nick was slightly startled, wondering how much they knew and how. He stared at Mary.

'You think you know everything? You know shit. Or are you jealous? You women are all the same, always pretending you're something you're not. She enjoyed everything we did to her and maybe you would too.'

Leann stood up. 'I think we are done here for a while. We're investigating this episode as we do not know how the victim died. When we do we may have to talk to you again, maybe down the station, so please do not leave town and if you can think of anything else, please call me as soon as possible.'

Leann handed him a card, and as he was leaving Mary interrupted his exit.

'Did you know she was pregnant with your child, and that she had an abortion last year?'

Nick turned around. 'No shit!' he said angrily. 'A life for a life eh? Now can I go for a drink? Thank you!' He stormed off without waiting for a reply and made his way back to the bar, kicking a chair on the way.

Leann sat back down next to Mary. 'What do you think?'

'Not what we expected, what happened to the good-looking charmer? I didn't like him, he's lying, not sure what about. He's given us enough to think that that's it, but there's more behind the bravado. He changed from being nervous and apprehensive to being arrogant, and that tells me that he went on the offensive to hide something. Did you see him flinch when you asked about the contaminated coke? He knows something, I'm sure.'

'I'm not sure I can arrest him for flinching, but I'm on the same page as you. He doesn't know we have his letters. They indicated that he was far more smitten by her than he just made out.'

'And his reaction to the pregnant comment, 'a life for a life', what do you make of that?'

'My view, I think he was really pissed off that he got dumped, and if he did know or has recently found out that she had an abortion that gives us a motive, doesn't it?'

'And why do you think she went for him?'

'I guess he was Top Cat in here, no worries, no responsibilities, exactly the opposite of what her life was. She could get out of her head and just enjoy herself. He does seem aggressive, but getting revenge by sending contaminated coke to her? I'm not sure, in fact I'm not sure that he could even think that far ahead.'

Mary pulled the photograph out again and studied it.

'What are you thinking now?' asked Leann

'Pretty women out walking with gorillas down my street.'

Leann recognised the lyric. 'Joe Jackson. I know what you mean.'

They left the bar and headed outside, saying thank you to Rebecca as they got to the door. They passed the smoking shed and got into their car. Four of five men were seated around Nick, no conversation, just staring at the two women.

'Let's get back, we've got to interview Kevin

tomorrow,' Leann said as she started the car. 'The guys out there are going to have a field day when Nick starts telling his story to them.'

'You think we should tell the drug squad? I really didn't like him,' said Mary.

'Not yet, we have enough to do. Let's see what happens over the next couple of days, then make a decision. I think he'll be going home tonight and getting rid of his stash anyway.'

'Don't ask me anything but I know someone, who knows someone, you know, someone else who can turn the heat up without that get backing to us.'

Leann smiled. 'Fine, let's do it, the heat is on.'

'On the street? Glenn Frey, great song, I think it was in *Beverley Hills Cop*?'

'I'll ask Cooper if he knows. Not sure his cinematic expertise extends to 1984 junk movies, but you never know with him.'

Leann started the car and slowly pulled away from the kerb, both of them glancing over to the smoking shed. Mary waved sarcastically. The short hop to the station should take them less than five minutes.

CHAPTER 24

BAD BOYS

It was almost 7pm, two hours after the ladies had left the Dog and Partridge and Pigeon, two hours for the bravado to come back and for Nick to retell his story several times, embellished each time, as different individuals stopped to say hello. Two hours for the two pints to turn into six.

Just as he was convincing the people around him that the police had no idea what was going on, describing them inaccurately as 'incontinent', a black

Range Rover with heavily shaded windows pulled up. The driver honked the horn twice, pulled away, drove round the block then parked ominously right outside the pub.

Nick had not seen the car, but he had heard the horn. He turned to Geoff, a painter who often shared an early afternoon beer with him before going home to his wife.

'What's Tariq doing here today? What day is it? It's not Friday.'

Geoff shrugged. He didn't really like Nick, but it was better than sitting on his own contemplating how to get rid of his nagging wife.

Nick downed his pint and waited, hoping the Range Rover would go away again. He was disappointed. As the car parked, he got up and walked past the wooden tables and benches, wiping his mouth and taking a deep breath. The passenger's electric window moved silently down. He was face to face with Tariq.

'Hey, what you doing here? It isn't Friday.' Nick tried to sound jovial, but he had a deep rumbling in his stomach, a feeling that something wasn't right.

'Just get in the back,' whispered Tariq.

'Er, I got some friends here, can I call you later?'

'Just get in the back.' A slightly more menacing tone.

'What is it, what's up?'

'Get in the fucking back, now!'

Nick pulled back from the window as it ascended and looked around, perhaps hoping Superman would turn up and whisk him away. He did another 360-degree check, opened the back door and climbed in. Before he could close the door, the car was moving. Nick acknowledged the driver for the first time; Tariq's younger brother Abu. Nick didn't know which country, religion or even continent they came from, but he had known them for five years, almost to the day. They had all met in a bar, Tariq and Abu picking Nick out of a crowd of guys on way to a football match in London. They recognised him as the type they were looking for, the gobby one, sniffing just a bit too hard. A few brief words about Brentford's latest manager, speculation on the score, and then an offer from Abu.

'Do you want some stuff to help you get through the game?'

'What sort of stuff?' Nick questioned.

'Just some lovely white powder, best in the area'

'How much?' Nick was keen.

Abu put his arm around Nick's shoulder and steered him towards the door.

'Price doesn't matter. You look like a decent guy, let's go outside and discuss.'

The deed was done in the alleyway behind the pub. Abu also give Nick a mobile phone number, which Nick entered into his phone.

'Any time, just call, we deliver, just like a local take-away.'

It started as an occasional call and quickly progressed to a fortnightly Range Rover drop every Friday, two toots of the horn, a quick trip around the block and a £200 transaction. Both Tariq and Abu knew that Nick sold on, but that didn't bother them. He probably couldn't work out if he sold for a profit or not. However this wasn't one of the scheduled Fridays, so it certainly wasn't a normal drop off.

Nick sat up straight, buckled up.

'Hey Abu, how are you?'

There was no answer. Instead of going around the block the car turned right onto the main road, left at the roundabout and then drove up a dirt track to a small farmhouse with a For Sale sign mounted at the gate. Abu switched off the engine, and an eerie silence descended.

Nick was nervously twitching in his seat. Tariq turned around.

'Well, my friend, a little birdie told me that you had some visitors earlier, two ladies?'

'God you're quick, how did you know?'

'My friend, it is not good to blaspheme, even if it isn't my God you are referring to.'

'Er, yeah, sorry.' Nick wasn't sure what blaspheme meant, but he realised he had said something wrong.

'So, my friend, when were you going to tell me? We had a deal that you had to stay clean else we pull out. We cannot afford to be associated with anyone that crosses that line. We run a respectable business that cannot, I repeat cannot, be compromised.'

'Er, yeah I know, it was nothing to do with you guys, that's why I didn't call. They just wanted to ask me some questions, honest.'

'Let me decide if it's anything to do with us. Tell me what questions.'

'OK, there's this lady that lived up the road who died recently, they were asking questions about her.' Nick didn't know how much to divulge.

'And this has something to do with you why?'

'Well like, I used to see her, hey actually you met her.' Nick was getting excited, 'She was at my birthday party last year, really attractive, blonde hair, great body, beautiful face, big tits.' Nick paused, trying to think of things that Tariq would remember about her. 'Pretty sure I introduced her to you, you said later that she was really nice.'

Tariq thought back. He had briefly attended a small get-together at Nick's flat, hoping to find another mug he could sell to. Everyone had been strung out on either coke or booze; he never touched either. He remembered meeting the lady, and could see she had a quality that Westerners would go for, but to him she was too loud, talked too much, wanted to be the centre of attention. He hadn't liked her.

'Go on,' he said.

'From what I know the police believe she died in suspicious circumstances, they don't know what of yet. That's all I know.'

'Not good enough, my friend. My sources tell me it might be a drug overdose, you know anything about that? Did those drugs come from you?'

Nick had a feeling that this wasn't going as well as he had hoped. His stomach rumbled again and he suddenly needed the toilet.

'Er yeah, er no, well I did give her some charlie when she wanted it, I never sold her any.'

'So the police want to talk to you because they know you provided the drugs.' Tariq had had enough of pleasantries. 'How?'

'I guess she told someone, but honest they didn't ask me where I got the drugs from, they said they weren't interested.'

Tariq's tone went up a notch.

'And you believed that? The police are talking to someone who has provided a Class A drug to someone who has died possibly from drug abuse and they don't want to know where it came from? Are you for real?'

Nick was getting defensive. 'That's what they told me, honest.'

Tariq took a deep breath and let out an audible sigh.

'Do you understand the phrase "supply chain"?' Nick looked blank. 'A supply chain is a system of organisations, people, activities, information and resources involved in moving a product from a supplier to customer. In this case you are a customer of mine; however I am a customer of someone else, you still with me?'

'Er yeah, think so.'

'So the police will want to know how far up the supply chain can they go with this incident. I will have to report this to my management as they cannot allow any breach in the supply chain, whatsoever.'

'I didn't mention your name, or Abu's, I wouldn't do that, I'm not a grass.'

'Of course you wouldn't, you would do time instead of mentioning our names, I am sure of that. Do you know why I'm sure of that? Because we know you, I mean really know you, and we know your family.'

Nick understood the threat. Tariq continued.

'If the investigation identifies the cause of death as a drug overdose, or drug contamination, then the police will come at you hard. Let me tell you, my friend, I will know about this before you. I think if this happens you might not be found by the police for them to follow up, you understand?'

'Er yeah, think so.' Nick's bladder was bursting. He just wanted to get out.

'Just so we are clear, I understand that you were not happy with her when she left you out in the cold. You didn't try to extract any revenge, did you?'

'I don't know what you mean,' Nick stammered.

Tariq had been staring at Nick throughout the conversation. He turned to Abu, gave him a slight nod and sat looking out of the windscreen. Then he said over his shoulder, 'My friend, I will not keep you any longer, so please get out of my car before you piss yourself on my leather seats.'

'What, here?'

'Yes here. You can think about what I said as you walk back, or even maybe find a way to plug the leak. Go, my friend, before I change my mind.'

As Nick unbuckled his belt and opened the door, Tariq returned the item he had taken from the glove compartment back to its hiding place. Nick thought he saw the handle of a gun, but wasn't sure. There were no pleasant au revoirs. Abu started the engine and gunned the car into reverse as soon as the door clicked.

Abu though Tariq had been a bit lenient, but he did not dare question his boss. Tariq twisted the rear-view mirror so he could see behind him. Nick was busy relieving himself into a bush. Tariq smiled and turned the mirror back.

'I think we just need to keep an eye on our friend. Let's go.'

CHAPTER 25

HELLO KEVIN

Leann picked up Mary the next morning and drove to Kevin's house, three houses down from where she and Cooper had gone previously for the first interview. They turned off the main road and onto the private road, snaking their way past parked Lexuses, BMWs and Jaguars.

'Nice place to live, nice houses, nice cars, lovely views. Must cost a bit round here,' said Leann.

'Yeah, the only way we are going to get this is if we win the lottery.'

'Or marry someone rich?'

'You wouldn't do that, would you? Compromise your integrity for money.'

'Everyone would do that, it's just how much, that's the question!'

Mary smiled. 'Maybe this Kevin will be the rich older man I could compromise my integrity for.'

'I guess we were wrong with our expectations yesterday, what about today?'

'From what you've told me so far about this saga, this man could have three arms and four ears and I wouldn't be surprised.'

Leann smiled. She liked Mary's straightforward sense of humour.

'Well we are here, so let's find out,' she said.

They pulled into a spacious drive and parked alongside a rather battered Ford Focus. In front of them was a large mock Tudor house, the white and black facade giving the place a slightly eerie feel. Two ginger cats were asleep by the porch in the early morning sun, but they soon jumped up and left as they heard the car doors open and close. Leann and Mary walked up to the porch.

'Did you ring ahead?' asked Mary.

'No, from what I have heard he's been a bit of a recluse of late, so I expect he's in.'

Leann pulled on the old-fashioned bell ringer and

they both stood back. The door opened slowly and a man's head poked around the door, unkempt grey hair, thick glasses surrounding a thin face with a prominent nose. His complexion was very pale, with the odd visible blood vessel. Small fox-like eyes peered through the glasses.

'May I help you?'

The officers had decided the previous night that they wouldn't wear their uniforms and were therefore dressed in civvies – dark trouser suits with light blouses.

'Good morning. We are looking for Kevin Blake?'

'Who are "we"?' he said, rather rudely.

'I am DS Leann Stuart and this is WPC Mary Abbott from Staines Police Station. Are you Kevin Blake?'

The man quickly scanned the ID proffered and opened the door wider.

'You'd better come in. Yes I am.'

He was dressed, or under-dressed, in a large woollen dressing gown and grey pyjama bottoms with no top, with an old pair of moccasins on his feet. A rusty pseudo-gold chain hung loosely round his neck and a similar bracelet adorned each wrist. He pulled the dressing gown closed so as not to reveal his body, led them through a dark hallway and gestured for them to come into the kitchen. Last night's take-away trays were stashed in the sink and a few empty bottles of wine were resting on the worktop. From the kitchen windows you could see a well-kept lawn which spread out, encompassing several full bushes before culminating at a small brick wall and leading from there past the towpath to the Thames flowing by.

'Apologies, please give me five minutes to get dressed,' said Kevin. It's a bit early for me, I'll put the kettle on first.'

He filled the kettle, turned it on and then left, his footsteps banging on the stairs as he ascended.

'Well that's a shock' whispered Leann.

'She certainly didn't go for good looks or personalities when she chose her men. Maybe that means something?'

'I think it does. Maybe she didn't want to leave at all and just chose men that didn't stand a chance.'

Mary leaned closer to Leann and whispered, 'or maybe they both had really big dicks'.

Leann stifled a cough and swallowed a laugh that eventually came out as a 'Hurmp'.

'I hope she kept her eyes closed.'

'Enough already' demanded Leann. Mary had a way of making lewd remarks at inappropriate times.

'Although I'm glad he pulled his gown together he looked like a prisoner of war, so skinny, chest covered with wisps of white hair, it reminded me of a dead rabbit I saw at the butchers yesterday. And his breath, it was like walking past Fullers' brewery .'

On the worktop, next to the kettle, was another wine bottle, half full and accompanied by a half-full glass. Leann picked it up.

'That's a decent Shiraz, not expensive but not your supermarket cheap plonk either. My guess this isn't left over from last night, it's just been poured.'

'On the wine just after nine… there must be a song with that lyric in it, just can't think of one.'

Footsteps descending the stairs reminded the two officers where they were. When Kevin entered the kitchen, he didn't look much better; he was wearing a sweatshirt that had seen better days and a pair of jeans that were falling off his waist. He hadn't combed his hair or washed. Obviously he was not a vain man.

'Tea? Coffee? Something a bit stronger?' he offered.

'No thanks, we're fine', replied Leann.

Kevin picked up his glass of wine and took a large slurp. Then he lit a rollup from a bunch of pre-rolled ones lying loose on the worktop and sat down at the kitchen table opposite from the two police officers.

'How can I help two lovely ladies like yourselves?'

Leann ignored that and ran through the preliminaries, confirming address, age, profession. As they had with Nick fifteen hours earlier, she outlined why they were there.

'It's about Mrs Donaldson, the lady who lived three doors down from you. You are aware that she died on Monday and your name has come up in our enquiries. We have reason to believe that her death might not have been as straightforward as first thought and therefore we are pursuing some lines of inquiry so that we can rule out various people with motive or opportunity. Now if you wouldn't mind, could you please tell us what you know.'

CHAPTER 26

AT HOME WITH KEVIN

Kevin took a sip of his wine. 'I've been living here for 50 years. Me and my ex-wife split up fifteen years ago, she went off with a painter, and my daughter's flown the nest. I live on my own, I have no police record, I don't need to work and my pension allows me to live with the best wine and the best company – me.'

He smiled strangely. Maybe it wasn't his first glass of the morning Leann thought.

'I met the lady in question at various social functions and street parties, with her husband and kids, watched the kids growing up. As you know they lived three doors down, so we bumped into each other quite a lot. In fact I was such a good neighbour I used to cut their grass, well the front bit that leads down to the river, I didn't used to go into their garden, not at the beginning anyway. She was very attractive. I used to watch her at night going to bed though their window, there's nothing illegal about that. Sometimes she would leave the curtains open as she changed for bed or went for a shower. I think she knew I was watching, I had a lot of fun with that.

'Then I got lucky. I had an old friend Charles, lived one down the other side, old bloke just over 90 years old and he needed attention. I knew his family well and I used to visit him every day. I suggested to them that he needed a carer to help run his house and look after him, cook his meals, clean the house, you know, that sort of thing. They agreed and asked if I knew anyone, as they would pay privately. It just so happened I did know someone. I had seen her in her uniform coming to and from work so I knew she was in that line of work, she looked mighty fine I must say. Anyway I approached her and offered her the job, told her about Charles and what I thought he needed and invited her to meet him and his family. Obviously Charles would have to agree but I can be very persuasive when I want something, learnt that working in the city you know, had a good job once, that's what gives me my pension.'

'Arrogant twat' was the thought that slipped into Mary's mind.

'She came over, and although Charles was anxious about having someone look after him, I persuaded him and his family to take her on, cash in hand, big pay rise for her. So she started working for Charles as a full-time assistant. I already knew she liked a drink as I had seen her several times staggering home from the pub at lunchtimes and evenings.

'Next phase was easy. She would go round Charles's at about ten to clean and prepare lunch and I would pop round about eleven. The first couple of weeks she didn't join in having a drink with us, she was very professional and cleaned and fussed around whilst Charles and me would sit smoking and enjoying a morning gin and tonic. Soon that 11 o'clock gin that I used to share with Charles became an 11 o'clock gin for the three of us. She would down tools and sit with us, chewing over the facts of life and local gossip. She would then make Charles lunch and go home. I would leave soon after, as Charles liked a nap at twelve. Around six in the evening she would pop over to give Charles his dinner and I would be there about seven. We would open a bottle of wine so Charles could have a glass with his dinner and then it seemed rude not to finish it off, so I asked her to help me to do that. She would help Charles into bed and we would stay for a couple of glasses before she left to go home.

'She was beautiful, intelligent, kind and considerate, and her husband didn't appreciate her. One night, instead of drinking at Charles's and then going straight home, I asked her to come back to mine. The wine had run out and I offered her a nightcap. Her mobile had been ringing and her husband had been texting wondering where she was, but she ignored it, agreed and came back to my house. We talked and played music and smoked. I loved the way the cigarette rested on her lips, her husband wouldn't let her smoke in the house so this was a luxury to her. She could relax, no kids to put to bed, no one to tell her to stop drinking or not to smoke. She knew she was in heaven, just where she wanted to be, and I wanted her here. Me and her were a team, inseparable.

'This started off as a weekly occurrence but soon became more and more frequent. I told her about my life and how lonely I was and she told me about her life, how lonely she felt – she even told me about an affair she had been having recently. She felt like she was trapped in a house of boys. It was depressing, she didn't want to grow old, she wanted to live her life. The evenings went on later and later. At first she wanted to get home to say goodnight to her kids, then if she was on her second bottle she wouldn't bother, not answer or even turn her phone off. Several times her husband came round and banged on the front door, asked her to come home. She looked at him and said she was just coming and don't embarrass her in front of her friends. I think he knew, he could see what I was thinking but he couldn't do anything to stop the inevitable.

'Then I had the best night of my life when she told me she loved me. It was my birthday but I had bought her several presents to celebrate, expensive Pinot Grigio, that's a lovely Italian wine, perfume, French obviously, and underwear, Calvin Klein, and the kicker was she told me to leave them at my house as they would be between me and her.

'One thing led to another, but I took my time. One night she was so drunk and it was after 2am so I suggested she stay on the settee. She duly obliged and crashed out. I sat down on the floor and spent the next couple of hours watching her sleep, staring at her beautiful breasts as they rose up and down. I remember trying to look up her skirt.'

He smiled at the two women and took a large gulp of wine.

'Then a week later I had some friends around and to get some privacy we went upstairs to my bedroom, and she fell asleep. I undressed her, and she didn't wake. I put her on the bed and played with her, and she still didn't wake. She stirred, wriggled and writhed under my expert hand.' Kevin spread out his hands and fingers, then brought them together, cracked his knuckles, stared up to the ceiling and closed his eyes. There was an awkward silence; he appeared to have gone to a fond memory to relive an important part of his life. Leann was just about to interrupt his reverie when Kevin started again.

'I used to play loud music outside the window so it could be heard from her bedroom. I knew she could hear it and I knew it made her think of me sitting here waiting for her.'

It was Mary who interrupted this Romeo and Juliet power play. 'So when did the husband find out?'

'Oh him, I felt a bit sorry for him, silly bugger. He must have caught us several times before he finally put two and two together, I even kissed her, I mean a proper kiss right in front of him and she told him that what he had seen was a peck on the cheek for a good friend. He even caught us one night, he must have slipped up the towpath and seen us. We were kissing in the kitchen and he must have spied us through the window. I never closed the curtains, maybe I wanted people walking past to see us, see how happy we were together. I remember he banged on the window, really angry, but we didn't let him in. I thought he might throw a brick through the window at one point.

Anyway she left soon after and went home but came back the next day for more. I don't know what she told him, didn't really ask.

'When he went away on business for a week I practically lived in her house, she gave me a key, just the kids weren't allowed to see me in the morning. So he must have known, I just thought he didn't care. She did tell me she lied to him about what was going on but she always came back for more. Why wouldn't she?'

Mary couldn't help herself. 'I can think of many reasons,' she murmured. She wasn't sure if the others had heard, but Leann's disapproving stare confirmed that she had.

Kevin ignored the comment and continued. 'I remember one time they had had a big fight and she came and stayed for a couple of days, it was heaven, we were together at last, I thought it would last forever. She had finally told her husband about me. We went out for lunch, met a few friends and I introduced her as my girlfriend. I know she wasn't happy about that. I brought the presents I had bought her and put them into my wardrobe in my bedroom - she had told me she was moving in. That evening she went ballistic, I still don't know why, she's never told me. She just went back home. She quit working for Charles and started ignoring me. I sent her texts and letters, bottles and bottles of wine. I followed her, how could she just throw away the most important thing in her life? What was she thinking? I gave up everything for her, why? Why? Why?'

Kevin reached for his glass, and although there was still a mouthful in it he topped it up. He regained his composure.

'Are you sure you don't want a drink?' he offered.

'No thank you.' Again Leann answered for both of them. Kevin was getting louder; maybe the wine was kicking in.

'Then she dies, ha ha, she took me to heaven and hell within six months and three months later she dies. Does that make me feel better or worse? It was bad enough when she told me about Nick and all the things she did with him, then dumped him, then she chose me. She had made her mistake and now together we could live a new life. All she had to do was leave her husband. Why didn't she? Can you tell me?'

Mary and Leann were staring wide-eyed. They could not believe the rant they had just heard.

Leann thought silence was the best retort and glanced at Mary, hoping she would feel the same.

'You can't tell me, can you? Now I'm ruined, my life is ruined, I wish it was me that died with her. Why did she die, how did she die? Can you tell me that much?'

'As I explained earlier, we are not sure and we are

following several possibilities' said Leann. 'We're waiting for post mortem reports, but there are no obvious signs so we're looking at possible poisoning.' Leann thought she had better cut this off or else they would still be here this evening. 'Now can you please answer a few questions?'

Kevin took another gulp of wine. 'Sure. Look I know what, why don't we go out for lunch, the three of us, my treat?'

Mary jumped in but kept her cool.

'Sir, this is a very serious matter. I don't think lunch in a public house is appropriate,' she said sternly.

'Sure sure. OK, just ask away.' The ranting had stopped and a calm had descended on Kevin.

'Firstly', started Leann, 'you said she gave you a key. Do you still have it? When did you last use it?'

'Course I still have it, I have everything that she touched, it's all put away safely. As for when I last used it, I can't remember. Sometimes I would sneak into the house when they were away just to smell her, there's nothing illegal in that as she said I could,' he quickly added. 'Or I would go round and put a bottle of wine in the fridge for her so I would know she was thinking of me and to remind her of all the great times. I'm sure she wanted to leave. Other times I would just take the key with me when I went out, just to help me remember. As I was walking home I would take it out and imagine that I was coming home to her, to us. It was like having her with me, in my pocket, I wanted to own her, body and soul.'

Kevin slipped back into his reverie and stared at the glass. The awkward silence returned, but this time Leann interjected quickly.

'Could you please tell us where you were last Monday?'

'I was at home, I'm pretty sure, don't think I have left the house for about a month now, can't see the point. I order my shopping on-line, I might be getting old but I used to be a whizz with computers, it's amazing what you can find and do on the internet.'

'Thank you. Is there anyone who can vouch for you?'

'Nope, you will just have to take my word for it, I am an honourable man.'

'I am sure you are' Lean replied with a hint of sarcasm. 'Well, that's all for now. I'm sure you have no intention of going anywhere whilst we sort out this issue. We will keep in touch.' Leann and Mary stood up to leave.

'You two can come around anytime you like. Next time let me know and I can make myself more presentable, maybe then we could do lunch, or I could cook for you?'

There was no reply. Kevin offered his hand at the door, which they both accepted reluctantly. Kevin shook Leann's hand first. He held Mary's hand just a little too long.

Kevin stood at the door watching them as they walked to the car.

Leann and Mary strapped themselves in and as Leann started the engine Mary took a tissue from her handbag and wiped her hands.

'Urgh, I would hate to think where his hands have been. Please tell me you will not bring me here next time!'

'So you don't want to marry him for his money then? Compromise your integrity? Let's go get a coffee, my treat.'

'OK, but let me wash my hands first.'

CHAPTER 27

GOD ONLY KNOWS

Thirty minutes later a grey Honda CRV pulled up in Kevin's drive; its single occupant climbed out, slamming the door shut. Chuck was just over 70, a well-groomed man, his small stature compensated by a not-so-healthy girth. Dressed well in a tweed jacket, jeans and loafers, supplemented by a cloth cap covering his grey hair, he looked the part of an English country gent. In fact, as his name suggested, he was from North America, in fact Canada, and had spent the forty years since his move to England clarifying that he wasn't a Yank, quite happily explaining the subtle nuances of his language versus the American dialect. He lived a few miles up the river, and had recently married into the American dream by bagging a sophisticated English rose, incidentally called Rose. Chuck had worked in the City for most of his latter employment and had met Kevin whilst enduring the daily commute from Staines to Waterloo Station and onto the City via the direct tube link, affectionately known as the 'drain'.

Living in close proximity, Chuck and Kevin had become friends, and since Chuck's marriage they had spent many a Sunday around Kevin's. If the weather was tolerable they would barbecue on the lawn looking out over the river with Kevin's stereo system playing light rock music through the lounge doors.

It was there that Chuck had first noticed the new lady in Kevin's life. He had been there through the initiation, the cultivation, the infatuation and the obsession, and he had been there for the triumphant devastation at the end of that journey. He frequently questioned Kevin's behaviour and pointed out that it was going to end in tears. Rose had also seen the escalation of the friendship and told Chuck that she wanted nothing to do with it; she had pointed out in a very English way that Chuck should envision himself in the husband's shoes as if she was having an affair with a neighbour. What would he feel like, especially when the children came round?

Chuck got the point and spent several evenings banging his head against a wall as he tried to convince Kevin, to no avail. The obsession stage was particularly painful for Chuck as he saw his best friend starting to unravel. The drinking became heavier, the behaviour more erratic, and in the end Chuck just left Kevin to his own devices. So getting a call from Kevin this morning asking Chuck to come over as soon as possible, bearing in mind that they hadn't spoken for a few months, was more of an irritant than a pleasure, but Chuck agreed, sensing that something was seriously off kilter.

Kevin opened the door as Chuck approached. 'Hey, thanks for coming over, you're looking great, come on in.'

Chuck could smell the booze on Kevin as he passed by him in the doorway and made his way to the kitchen. A glass of wine was on the side, an empty bottle next to a newly-opened bottle, and two empty coffee cups on the table. It didn't take years at a detective school to work out that there had been visitors recently.

'I wish I could say the same about you,' Chuck replied. When Kevin's expression indicated that he didn't know what Chuck was talking about, he explained. 'Looking good - I wish I could say that you were as well, but you look like shit man, if you'll pardon my language.'

'You want a glass?'

'No thanks, Kevin, far too early for me, plus I have loads of things to do later. Rose and I are off to the Garden Centre, we have resculpted the front lawn. You'll have to come round and see what we're doing.'

'Yes, of course, I'd love that, I haven't been out of the house for a while. You don't mind if I do?'

Kevin topped up his glass and indicated to Chuck to sit down.

'Like I said, thanks for coming round, you'll never guess... wait, I'm forgetting my manners, how is Rose? She's not happy with me, I think. Not sure what I did to upset her, but please send her my regards.' Without waiting for Chuck to answer, he went on, 'Anyway, I had some visitors this morning, two very attractive police ladies called round. I think I have been very stupid.'

Chuck thought that no response would be the best course of action.

'Well, they wanted to talk to me about my girlfriend.'

'You still seeing her? I thought you had split up.'

'I don't think we split up, I think she just wanted a

short break before she left her kids and husband. She told me we would be together, so I was waiting for her. I still have all her stuff upstairs.'

'So what's happened that's brought the cops round?'

Kevin paused and finished off his glass of wine.

'She's dead. She's left me, left me all alone, after all her promises,'

Chuck sat up and interrupted.

'Whoa man, did you say she's dead? Is that physically dead or metaphorically dead, I mean dead as in died?'

'Yes, dead, dead as in not alive. She died at home a few days ago. The police are doing an autopsy. They think she might have been poisoned, or took an overdose, or something, they didn't really say.'

Chuck got up from his seat, reached up on to one of the cupboards above the sink and pulled out a glass. Then he took the bottle of wine from the worktop and poured himself a full measure. He took a large swig and starred out of the window watching the Thames flow serenely by, collecting his thoughts.

'Now I know why you wanted me to come over. So the police came round asking if you knew her, what she was like?'

Chuck turned around to see that Kevin was crying into his wine.

'Chuck, why did she leave me? She promised, how could she do that to me?'

Chuck was taken back. 'It's not all about you. Think of her kids, her husband, how do you think they feel?'

Kevin just sobbed. Chuck looked away, letting the moment pass, waiting for Kevin to pull himself together.

'You know she was my life, and now it's all over,' Kevin went on.

'You said you did something stupid, what have you done?'

'I didn't kill her, if that's what you're thinking, I wouldn't do that, but I have done some stupid things.'

'Like?'

'Well the police asked if I had been round her house.'

'And you obviously haven't, have you?'

'I did, several times, I used to bring her bottles of wine and put them in the fridge when the house was empty, and sometimes I would take some of her clothes, just for keepsakes, nothing morbid.'

'But you didn't tell the police that and you're worried that they will find your fingerprints?'

'Not exactly, I did tell the police, they were very nice about it.'

Chuck thought for a moment. 'So the police have a dead body, possibly poisoned, and you have admitted to being round the house, stealing clothes, providing wine – anything else?'

'I did write a few letters, not threatening, just wanted her to know how I felt and how I couldn't live without her.'

'That's great, man.' Chuck was getting more and more exasperated, he couldn't help himself. 'We did try and tell you, you just wouldn't listen. Shit creek and paddle come to mind.'

'But I didn't do anything!'

Chuck finished his glass. 'If I remember rightly the last time you called me you said something to the effect "if she won't live with me then she ain't going to live with no one else" and "if she ain't coming back I will give her something of a surprise". You recall that conversation?'

'Not really, I was pretty angry then.'

'So what's changed to make you less angry? You've been stewing in your own meatloaf for the past couple of months.'

'But I didn't do anything, honest.'

'Look I believe you, there's nothing you could have done. What do the police think, you put bleach in the wine bottle or something?' Chuck's inflection indicated sarcasm, but Kevin looked up startled, the last bit of colour drained from his face.

'No, no, no, why would I do that? I wouldn't, you have to believe me, I would tell you if I had.'

'You wouldn't tell me Kevin, because you know I would tell Rose. We have no secrets between us, and what she would do with that information God only knows. Gee Kevin, how dumb have you been?'

CHAPTER 28

LEANN AND MARY

On their way home the two officers stopped for a coffee at the Starbucks on the high street. Leann forked out for both hers and Mary's speciality, Caramel Macchiato; as it was just before lunch the tables were relatively free, the wait for the barista to top the coffee with the caramel wasn't long and they were soon sitting down in the corner. Mary got up, looked at her hands rather dramatically and headed off to the restrooms. A few people looked up to see what had come in and disturbed their routine, but they soon returned to their newspapers, PCs and smart phones.

'So now what do you think?' Leann challenged Mary on her return.

Mary sat down and took the first sip of her drink. 'The coffee's not as hot as it should be and it could have done with some more of the sugary stuff on top.'

'Not the coffee!'

Mary smiled, 'I know, dummy'. There was no regard for seniority when they were out like this.

Mary took another sip of her coffee. 'I guess you brought me along to get another perspective, so now I have had the pleasure' she sneered, 'of meeting both of them, this is how I see it. I have a delicious and complete disdain for both of them. Nick is a pseudo hard man, full of testosterone and claims to be the big guy "in de hood", but I think she got under his skin; she was his uptown girl and he was the bit of rough. Only trouble was the uptown girl knew that bit of rough wouldn't be able to keep uptown girl in the manner she was accustomed to, so he eventually got dumped before she got thrown out of her house. I don't believe he knew she was pregnant, or that she had an abortion, at the time, but I do think he found out, maybe quite recently.'

She paused and took a larger gulp from the coffee mug.

'I'm speculating that in the beginning he kept it quiet, no one was allowed to know, but that changed, he invited his mate. It's like that joke about being stuck on a desert island alone with Johnny Depp, it's not worth anything unless you can tell someone. Once the news got out it spread like wildfire and he was king dick. Then when it all went south he was left with egg on his face, big time. It's a thin line between love and hate - wasn't that a song?

'Yep, Chrissie Hynde or The Pretenders, can't remember which.'

'Now he is really pissed off and tries to keep in contact but to no avail, he sends her sweeteners, things to remind her of him and the good times. This will certainly affect her, from what you told me so far. If she is that partial to a snort, depressed and feeling trapped, then it might be a good way to make the day go faster, easier. If he was that pissed off then I wouldn't put it past him to send a special present added to the sweetener, maybe something to make her sick added to the cocaine. It's not difficult, I understand. How angry would you be if you found out that your girlfriend had aborted your child without even asking you? Obviously I'm not a man, so I can't speculate with any accuracy.'

She paused again, took another slug. 'Mmmm, this is good coffee.'

Leann remained silent, quietly sipping.

'As for the other tosser, I know I have a low threshold in men but even I don't stoop that low,' Mary went on. 'Maybe charming if you're an alcoholic and can't see further than your nose. He was the opposite to Nick, the father figure extraordinaire, buying presents, manipulating her into believing her life with him would be a lot smoother. But it sounds like he really lost it when she left. He certainly did not understand why. He had the opportunity, with a key to the house, and no alibi that he, or we, can corroborate. What if he just popped by on the Monday, would she let him in? He admits he watched the house, so he would know she was in all alone. He brings some wine around, contaminated with something? He helps to get her more wasted than she already was and then leaves, knowing she would continue drinking? Does he have the balls or is he that insane, was that a show just for us? It's so nice to be insane, no one asks you to explain.'

'Helen Redding I think, *Angie Baby*?'

Mary thought for a while.

'I noticed in your notes that during the interview our victim had a 'Truth Day' when she coughed up all the dirty laundry, told the old man everything, warts and all. However today this Kevin claims that she had been sleeping with him for six months, but on Truth

Day she stated three months. Was she still lying? Is there anything else that doesn't match up? I don't know what difference it makes but if one part of the story isn't correct how much of the rest of it do you believe?'

Leann digested what Mary had said, and made no comment. They finished their coffees.

'How can we prove any of this?' asked Mary.

'We can't. I brought you along for your intuition, not the facts, I can get anyone to do that bit. Tell me what you feel.'

'You're waiting to ask me the billion-dollar question, which one is the more capable.'

'Right.'

'That's easy to answer. I have spent all this time in the police force, and added to that I have my unique intuition, and together they have provided me with unparalleled capability in the power of deduction. If I could, I would bet my house on this answer. I have no idea, not the foggiest. It could be one or the other or both.'

CHAPTER 29

BUGGER'S MUDDLE

Cooper and Leann broke for a comfort break, having digested her reports of the previous day's meetings with Kaz, Nick and Kevin. They had taken notes, questioned each other, questioned themselves and now needed to think over what they had got, to summarise and conclude. After a wash, a wee and some water, Cooper was staring into space when Leann re-entered the room.

'So what now?' she asked.

'That's exactly what I was thinking.'

'Seems like a real mixed bag we need to start sorting through,' Leann said, sitting down. 'I think I could use a drink now, never mind later.'

'At times like this we need to focus and get facts, else we could be running around chasing our own arses for days.' Cooper smiled. 'OK, your thoughts.' He sat back.

Leann stood up, walking around the room to help herself concentrate.

'Let's assume for now that someone wanted to kill her. Then we have Nick, Kevin, Joe or persons unknown. Nick certainly acted surprised when I mentioned she had been pregnant, and I'm sure he flinched at the mention of contaminated drugs. He seemed violent, although he has little previous. He was cautioned for a domestic dispute that got out of hand a couple of years ago, and his change in behaviour after he got dumped was obviously significant. Let's assume he was really pissed off that he was dumped, tried to win her back any way he could, sent her some coke to remind her of the good times. She didn't respond, nought, nada... then he finds out that she had had an abortion, assume he found out in the last couple of weeks, somehow. Certainly he now has motive, but not opportunity, unless he contaminated the drugs himself and then sent them to her, knowing that if she had a bad day she would turn to the coke to get over it.'

Cooper listened intently.

'Does he have anything to gain?' she went on. 'Not really – self-satisfaction, if I can't have you then no one can? Wasn't that in one of the letters? I know it's a bit weak, but I guess its threatening? Then he just drops some duff coke around, she takes it as she can't be arsed to do anything else – the therapist mentioned that when she lost it she really lost it –and hey Joe, she's lying dead. That, sir, is scenario One.'

Cooper looked up and motioned for her to continue.

'Scenario Two, let's look at Kevin. Well he certainly has opportunity, a key to the house - he's admitted to visiting frequently when he shouldn't be. Nothing illegal in that, as he said himself several times. He was very upset, seemed like it was his last chance of happiness, and then she ruined it by going back to the husband. I'm a bit perturbed about the wine – the husband mentioned a different brand from the one he found. Kevin mentioned that he bought her expensive wine. Could he have doctored the wine, added something to it, reclosed the lid and dropped it off? Or even gone round with it? Would she have realised that the wine had been previously opened? What did Kevin have to gain from her death - couldn't he stand the sight of her any more as she had destroyed their lives together? Is he angry enough? I think so.'

Cooper interrupted. 'Out of the two?'

Leann thought a while. 'Both the same. I see deep anger in both, I don't get the actual connection from her to both of them, they both had something they thought they wouldn't have and then she just pushed them away, why?'

'Maybe they knew each other and planned this together?'

Leann shot Cooper a despairing look. 'Let's not go there, we have enough loose ends. We know they know each other, we know they both know that they both knew her, does that make sense? But as a collaboration?'

Cooper sighed. 'I have seen worse collaborations between two people, Kermit and Miss Piggy, De Vito and Schwarzenegger in *Twins*, even Sweeney Todd and Mrs Lovett.'

'What are you talking about?'

'Just educating you, don't worry before your time. Just thinking out loud.'

'So no.' Leann shrugged. 'I don't see it as collaboration or a coming together of likeminded people, not even as a possibility, actually.'

CHAPTER 30

THREE'S A CROWD

'Then we get to Scenario Three' Leann continued, 'which is the husband either bumps her off or pays for someone to bump her off. What's your take on that one sir?'

'Right, his whereabouts that day are confirmed. He wasn't near the house all morning, or lunchtime. CCTV picked him up at the station getting off the London train at 2.30. We know he got on the train in the morning and we know he was in London having lunch with a potential employer from twelve till one, although I don't think that firm will offer him a job after we had to speak to him. He arrived at school to pick the boys up shortly before three o'clock, which is a fifteen-minute drive, no hope of him going home first, and he found the body just after three-fifteen, so unless he's the invisible man, or has a stunt double, then he had no opportunity. If he paid someone off then we would need to look at financial records and see, but even if he did, who would he pay? Someone who knew her, obviously. There was no struggle or break in, no sign of anybody else in the house at the time, neighbours didn't see anyone.'

'What about him collaborating with Nick, Kevin or both?'

Cooper gave her a withering stare. 'Touché, but let's not go there as we didn't go for the collaboration angle for just Nick and Kevin. To go for, pardon my expression, another threesome, would really stretch the imagination. Before we started today the only threesomes I knew where the Three Stooges and Athos, Porthos and Aramis.'

Leann gave him that quizzical look again.

'Could we include Alvin and the Chipmunks?'

'Yep, heard of them.'

Leann smiled back, and Cooper continued.

'Therefore my dear,' he said rather dramatically,

'we are left with no opportunity and no motive, but we do have a body. If we can establish motive then we can work out how.' He thought for a moment. 'What about those letters, could he have found them recently? Would that make a difference?'

'I don't think so, sir. He said he had found them a couple of months back and to be honest they didn't really deviate from the story she had told him and he already knew. There were some pleas to get back together, but it was all one sided, as far as I could see.'

'Maybe there were more letters that he hasn't shown us, or thrown away, that describe the situation more vividly, or even a film. You know you can do that on a phone these days.'

'Sir, what difference would any of that make? You think that would make him flip? He knows, he's been told and told again. There isn't anything a letter or a film or anything, nothing could be much worse than he's gone through, and still he stuck by her. The question is, why? Is his love that blind, stupid or just misdirected?'

'OK, just trying to find an angle, something that could lead us down a road. Let's recap. If we look at the toxicology report, we were given three possibilities. Therefore if he was wanting to 'bump her off' as you so eloquently put it, then he would have had to have found the drugs and/or the wine and doctored both.

Nick admits to sending drugs and Kevin admits to sending her wine. Could we just have a lucky case that Nick sent some contaminated drugs to scare her and to show that she shouldn't have left him, Kevin pissed in her wine to get his own back because she dumped him and it just happens she takes both on the same day? Is that too coincidental?'

'That is a stretch I agree, but not impossible.'

'Then there is no case. If we put anyone on trial for this and the defence can put together a strategy that, as preposterous as it sounds, this could all have been a pissed-up, drug-sodden coincidence with less chance of happening than I have of winning the lottery, then again there is diddly-squat, zip.'

'Let's call it a night, we can reconvene in the morning, we have a call with the Super at nine thirty when we will present our best case, which at the moment is no case. Maybe we should ask for more time. Or most likely after all our work we will be re-assigned. Now go get some shut eye.'

'OK.' Leann picked up her bag. She didn't need to be told again. She was tired, and it had been a long and taxing week. After they had swapped good nights, Leann made her way out of the office, through the long corridors, into the fresh air and into her car. 'Home in fifteen minutes tops' she murmured to herself.

CHAPTER 31

HELLO

Leann hauled herself out of the bath; the water was now lukewarm, which was to be expected after two hours of lathering and soaking, accompanied by a touch of shuteye. She wrapped a towel around herself, pink and fluffy, and tucked the end under her left armpit. The house was quiet, but she was getting used to that. Will had walked out over six months before; well 'walked' wasn't really the truth, she had pushed him out, slowly, one bit at a time, so he would think it was his decision. He was a nice enough guy, and nice guys deserve better, but she had been in a relationship for six years with him, living together for the last two, and over the last six months she had planned his exit. It wasn't anything specific, although Will still wouldn't accept that. She justified it as evolution; the cogs that turned together to make their relationship work had started getting rusty and in her mind her cogs had stopped. She wanted more time at work, more time to think and more space to live in. She didn't want to start seeing someone else, although she had had plenty of offers, mainly from people within the force; she wanted to be her own person. She had realised in the last six months of the relationship that Will was hanging on to a belief that she didn't share, and that was bringing her down.

Anyway, she had now got used to the quiet house, with every creak and groan of the old floorboards echoing around the bathroom. She walked towards the wardrobe, stopping in front of the full-length mirror, took her towel off and wrapped it around her hair, pinning it up as only women can do. She checked her breasts for lumps, a daily routine, ever since her mother had died from the consequences of lumps which had been found too late, a year before her death. It had been two years, this daily check, but it was by no means morbid, rather a sort of celebration of her mother's life. Her mother had made her promise to check daily (don't do what I did, do what I say), and now the ritual brought back the good times spent with mum.

All in order she stood in front of the wardrobe and drew back the door. What to wear? She glided through the bedtime choices, sexy silky tops and shorts, mainly bought by Will, long comfortable satins from high street stores bought for her by her friends, remnants of cotton pyjamas from Marks and Spencers, courtesy of her dear mother, and at the end a new onesie bought by herself after Will had left. She had splashed out; not one of those cheap ones available only three months before Christmas but a fully-fledged single-purpose body comforter. She had even had her initials embroidered on the left part of her chest, 'L.O.'

'L.O.' used to be the bane of her life. School life would have been better if no one had picked up on it and its phonetic neighbour, 'Hello'. It had stuck with her until Jennifer Lopez came on the scene, when she was affectionately known as J. Lo for a while. However, her father also picked up on the Hello reference, being old enough to remember the black and white television series *Dixon of Dock Green*, the eponymous hero being Constable George Dixon, a mature and sympathetic character who opened every episode with the inimitable 'Good evening all' but was more synonymous with his familiar phrase 'Hello hello hello', used whenever he came across a situation that required some attention. Since her father's Alzheimer's had taken hold not long after her mother's death and the remarkable coincidence that Leann had joined the police, he almost always greeted her with 'L.O. L.O. L.O.' and then painstakingly explained the obvious. Still, as it was her father, she would laugh and pretend she had never heard it before.

With a feeling of contentment, and no sense of sexiness, Leann made her way to the double bed that occupied most of the master bedroom. In this case the term was a euphemism for the only bedroom; still, it was hers, another thing that had bothered Will. The two up, two down Victorian terrace was all hers, her mortgage, her choice, her furniture. She could understand why Will wanted to change things, but she stuck firm. Now the spare box room was a walk-in wardrobe and ironing centre, the kitchen/diner was sparsely stocked, as take-aways were her favourite food, and the living room was home to a large flat screen television, a two-man sofa bed from IKEA (just in case anyone wanted to stay), a desk for work and a few bookshelves.

Her bedroom contained her prize possession, a Bang and Olufsen 9000, one of the Danish company's top of the range compact disc players, providing

.rt to anyone who could appreciate it. Costing
, much as the system and stacked neatly on
⌐ .ves mounted on the wall (thanks Will), sorted in
alphabetic order was Leann's eclectic music collection,
from A-Ha to ZZTOP and plenty in between. From the
vast collection she selected two CDs. One was Phil
Collins's *Face Value*, written after his messy split from
his first wife, full of mournful lyrics sitting above the
distinct drumming finesse. The second album was also
carefully selected for the mood she wanted to be in;
Robert Cray's *Strong Persuader*, the blues guitarist at
his most melancholic. With the shuffle button pressed
she wandered off to lie on the bed, anticipating what
track the random selector would choose.

As the opening bars of Collins's *In the Air Tonight*
reverberated gently towards her eardrums, she picked
up a pad and pencil from the bedside table and lay
down. She wanted to get in the zone. She liked looking
at puzzles from different angles, feeling the empathy,
letting herself drown in another person's frame of
reference; this case had been a tough tale of woe, but
there was something absent, a trigger, a spark, she
didn't know what. She wanted to find out if she could
feel the pain, identify the source and define the
missing link. Only then she could know who was
innocent and who was not.

As the drums kicked in, she wrote down all the

people involved, shut her eyes and started doodling, squares and circles, lines as squiggles, most random, some joining up at certain tangents. Leann thought of Cooper, a good copper but a copper just the same, old school, by the book, look for evidence, find a motive, nail a suspect. Her modus operandi was more ethereal: 360-degree view, all sides, above and below, and then piece the sums together. Her view was that the biggest problem in this case, besides the fact that the victim was dead, was the motive. If they assumed that one of the three protagonists were guilty of some offence, which was the most likely and why? Cooper would have spotted the obvious, but she needed to look around the edges, what was current, what was happening now.

Leann looked down at her pad as Robert Cray started singing about a smoking gun. Just what she wanted. Her doodles were difficult to understand but in between the long and short pencil strikes a definite oblong box emerged, and inside a smaller square at the top, with several little boxes in some sort of linear arrangement - a mobile phone? The thought stuck in her head. Had she discussed with Cooper a possible film, a trophy? Would one of the guys actually film their night, or nights, of passion? And then was it distributed? Could that have been the trigger?

She considered the effect – who would take the

film, who was in it, who had seen it, why now. The permutations were endless, and her thoughts zipped in different directions. If someone sent her a film clip, or an internet link, threatening to tell her husband, what would she do? She was obviously fragile of mind. A clip of a new episode that he didn't know about, blackmailing her to get back together... what if the husband saw it or if she told him? Would she tell him? Would Leann tell her partner if something like that happened? Will, although very laid black and placid, would have hit the roof, but would she have told him? Definitely not.

She reached for her laptop on the bedside table. Then, using her Wi-Fi, she logged into the net, loaded up a search engine and started wondering what to type. She had previously entered her name and got no hits at all, from 'unfaithful wives in Staines' to generic. In a separate investigation she had come across a local swingers' club. She had initially thought it had something to do with traditional jazz and was rushing to tell Cooper that this was right up his street, but luckily she hadn't.

Phil Collins was asking 'why can't it wait till morning' as she keyed in the club name 'ABRA' and looked at the website. There was a photo gallery, good place to start. Browsing through pictures of half-naked men and women in various poses and positions did nothing for her; this was work. She looked at group photos, individual photos, long shots, close-ups, but no faces were recognisable. The search seemed impossible, but then Leann came to a close shot of a bald man facing away from the camera, his right hand holding a clump of blonde hair, with the accompanying face pressed into his hip. He was either fully naked or naked from the waist up. There was no way you could identify either person, but Leann looked closer; for some reason she was drawn to this picture. The man's left arm was clearly visible. When she increased the size of the photo she recognised the tattoo. She had seen it before. At last she had a lead.

She closed down her laptop. She had something. It wasn't illegal to go to swingers' clubs, but it was something that Nick hadn't told them. Had he taken Kate Donaldson to ABRA? It certainly could be her against his hip. If there was a photo, there could be a film. She would tell Cooper in the morning; she was sure he would raise his eyebrows when she explained her thought process to him. Nick – she didn't like him.

Leann turned off the lights, put away her pen and pad and got herself comfortable. The music was often left on; she liked going to sleep to music, though Will hated it. There was another thing they didn't have in common. Robert Cray had just started singing about a neighbour having an affair:

I can hear the couple fighting right next door

Angry words sound clear through these thin walls

Around midnight I heard him shout "unfaithful woman"

And I knew right then the axe was gonna to fall

It's because of me, it's because of me

Because of me, it's because of me.

Her last thoughts before she fell asleep were not of Nick but of Kevin.

CHAPTER 32

JIGSAW DINOSAUR

They met at the door to the office they had vacated the night before. Cooper had an uncanny knack of knowing she was just about to open the door and beating her to it. Two cups of coffee were steaming away on the table as she took her seat.

It was half an hour before the call with the Super; the conference phone was positioned in the centre of the table. They would call the number, connect through the speaker phone and the Super would be there listening to their investigation and then making a decision, one way or the other. Options were simple; either continue investigating or not. Leann and Cooper had to convince the Super they had enough to pursue, else they would be re-allocated. Every day there was a different priority and the Super was the resource juggler.

She waited until Cooper had sat down and asked the obligatory question.

'You sleep well?'

'I did thank you, and you?'

'Not so bad. I'm sure as my wife gets older her snoring gets louder, but who am I to complain about the finer things in life?'

They both took a minute to have a drink. Cooper was aware that Leann wanted to tell him something.

'So what is it?' he started.

'Well, I was thinking last night...'

Leann went on to explain her thought process, her on-line investigation and her assumptions and to outline a new scenario. As she expected, when she explained about the ABRA website Cooper's eyebrows lifted, but he didn't ask any questions.

'So you think that maybe Nick took her to a swingers' club, maybe someone took a film, she never told anyone, Nick then came out with the film blackmailing her to get back together, she says no... is that it?'

'Well, now you come to look at it in the cold light of day it does seem a bit flimsy,' Leann conceded. 'Last night I was pretty sure there was something in it. We could subpoena Nick's phone or computer, if he has one, and check. That would give us motive.'

'On what grounds?' Cooper challenged.

'Jealousy, blackmail, accessory to murder, even use the drug angle and start looking deeper. I am pretty sure he knows more than he's letting on.'

'I agree.'

'You agree?' This time both of Leann's eyebrows lifted. 'You agree that we should have a go at Nick?'

'That is not what I said. I agree that he knows more than he is letting on. As for how we can use our cunning intuition to persuade the Super to let us look closer, I'm not so sure, and if you can't convince me then you have no hope with the Super.'

Leann sat back. She knew Cooper was right; intuition doesn't often pay the bills.

'Look, I admire the way you think, how do you say 'outside of the packet'?

'The box, outside the box, blue sky thinking, you must have heard of those terms before?'

'Sure, sure, outside the box, but in my experience the Super will look for evidence, not speculation. What actual evidence do we have?'

'You're right. You know I like working with you,

although you are a bit of a dinosaur.'

Cooper smiled. 'The feeling is mutual. Not that you're a dinosaur, but I do enjoy working with you, you bring a certain uncertainty to the proceedings. He paused. 'No matter what happens in this call we have done a thorough job. I just feel this time the jigsaw had too many missing pieces.'

They both looked at the clock as the minute hand crept to the six. Leann reached for the phone to dial the teleconference number, then looked at Cooper and smiled.

'Remind me again, what's a jigsaw?'

CHAPTER 33

END OF CHAPTER

Cooper and Leann arrived at my place unexpectedly, when the boys were back at school. As I opened the door I realised they were alone; I think I was expecting more than just the two of them. They had my computer with them, and they weren't smiling. I wasn't sure what these thoughts would add up, to but I somehow knew a decision had been made.

I invited them in, sat Cooper and Leann at the kitchen table and offered them a cup of tea. Had it only been five days since they first came round? I had spent the last half hour doing nothing, and I mean nothing. I was sitting with the radio on in the lounge and had cleared my mind. This was a new thing for me. I was usually obsessed with doing something and found it hard to sit still, but recently that had changed. I knew I had lots to do, people to see, places to go, a funeral to arrange but I hadn't started on that list yet.

No one talked until the tea was set down and the first sips taken.

Cooper started. 'Thanks for seeing us uninvited, I hope we are not disturbing you?'

I guess my silence was taken as an invitation to continue.

'Well, it's like this; we have had preliminary reports on the toxicology test and reports from the pathologist. We have spent the last five days talking to everyone who could be involved in this, er... incident over the last couple of years. It's not been pretty for sure and I think we have stirred up a bit of a hornet's nest, so expect the neighbour's tongues to be wagging.'

I sipped my tea and gave him a look that hopefully meant 'go on'.

'We have concluded that the deceased died in unusual circumstances. How unusual is the problem we have.'

I wasn't sure if I was meant to interject at this point so I remained silent.

'The reports show some suspicious substances in Mrs Donaldson's bloodstream, namely bleach and rat poison, but we cannot determine how they got there. The toxicologist suspects that the rat poison was administered as part of the cocaine she had taken that morning and the bleach had been mixed with wine. We have statements from people you may know who have both admitted to providing wine and coke to your wife, although both deny contaminating either. They also deny supplying anything recently.'

I sat breathing evenly. I wasn't sure what emotion I should show, so I tried to look quizzical and surprised.

Cooper went on, 'Your late wife also had a seriously deteriorating liver and there was vomit in her lungs. The latter is expected with the contaminating substances, but according to the pathologist she should have been able to expel the vomit if she had wanted to.'

He took a long sip of his tea.

'As we have no sign of forced entry, no sightings of people visiting and alibis for most of the witnesses for the day in question, we must deduce that your wife willingly took these drugs and the wine, either knowing or not knowing that they were not what they seemed.'

He stopped again and asked if I had any questions.

I shook my head and waved them to go on.

'We spent a long time last night going through the evidence and then this morning we met with the Crown Prosecution Services, so please accept our apology if we look a little jaded.' I hadn't noticed that. I remained silent, although I realised I had stopped breathing. I quickly reached for my cup and took a long drink.

'So, our evidence points to a number of scenarios, but most of these are just conjecture. To be honest we believe that the deceased was harmed by someone, possibly more than one person, who provided doctored substances, but that she took them willingly. The CPS went through each scenario that we described and asked a lot of questions. They concluded that as we have no clear evidence or motive, we cannot arrest anyone. I know this must sound, well... incomplete, but unless something else comes up or some new evidence comes to light, we are concluding this case. The deceased's body will be released to the mortuary this afternoon and you can arrange the funeral.'

I felt he did know what to say but had to do the formalities.

We all sat in silence whilst I assimilated the information I have been given. I looked at Leann, the first time I had really looked at her since they had arrived. She was wearing a silk blouse under a nicely tailored jacket which showed off her figure, and I admonished myself for having that thought.

As she spoke I looked away. Her voice was softer than I remembered from our previous conversations.

'Do you understand what you have been told, and are there any questions?' she said.

I stood up and paced around the room for a moment. I then decided that I needed to summarise what they said and conclude the conversation.

'So basically, you believe my wife was murdered. But you can't prove anything, no motive, and you have talked to everyone you can but no one is coming forward to say I did it? However it seems that she might have committed suicide, knowing that someone had supplied coke and wine that might have been doctored, and she just gave up? And the person or people who supplied these substances can be traced, but not enough evidence is there to prove that they had intention to harm or even if they had been the person who altered the substances?'

They remained silent, leaving me to go on. I wondered if I was supposed to go into a rage and demand to know why the perpetrators had not been more thoroughly questioned, or even tortured, but I think this would have been misplaced anger and not productive.

'I take it this goes down as suspicious

circumstances, but effectively death by misadventure,'
I went on. 'So that's that then, end of chapter.'

CHAPTER 34

WIVES KNOW BEST

It had been a long couple of days, and evenings, so Cooper dropped Leann off at the station, then phoned his wife and told her to expect him home for dinner. She was immediately upbeat and suggested they should get a take-away and eat together.

He opened the front door to the powerful aroma of fresh Chinese, took off his coat, jacket and tie and made his way to the kitchen. He had deliberately left his laptop and bag in the car, locked away in the boot, feeling that if he didn't bring it inside he would not be tempted to work. His mission tonight was to relax and forget about everything.

That didn't last long. Half way through their dinner he looked at Jean and smiled. Although she was nearly sixty she still looked great, and it wasn't only Cooper who said so. Her blonde hair was drawn back, showing some of the greying strands that would normally be hidden when they went out. She was dressed comfortably, but he could still see her curves and knew they hadn't changed much in the last 35 years. Even after having two kids who had now flown to freedom, she had kept trim and still looked great. Her smile lit up the room. You couldn't spend that long together and not know each other. Or could you? After the Donaldson case he couldn't believe how much one partner in a marriage could fail to know about the other. The infidelity was particularly hard for him. His own eyes had wandered over the past 35 years, but his hands and lips had remained faithful.

'Go on' she said. 'I know you want to tell me.'

He laughed gently. Could she really read his mind?

'Ok, get ready for a saga and a half' he said, and started to talk. His wife listened intently, never once interrupting.

Cooper concluded, 'So we can't charge anyone. It has to be death by misadventure, although I'm sure I am missing something. I'm leaning towards the husband, but I can't find the missing bit.' He sat back, waiting for her to respond.

'So after all those years the husband had put up with just about all he could,' she began. 'On one occasion he hit her, and after that all he did was take her back time and time again, for the sake of the family. Sounds very traditional. She must have been very screwed up. Have you thought what could possibly give him a motive to kill her now, after all this time? For the last three years he had lived with it, so why now?'

'That's what I don't understand. If he'd killed her when she came home pregnant he'd probably be out by now.'

Jean sighed. Sometimes the simplest things are right in front of our eyes, but we can't see them. What do you think the most important thing is for this man?'

'Being happy, having the family together, protecting the kids…'

'There's your answer, right in front of your nose.'

'What? Protecting the kids?'

'The key word is 'the'.'

Cooper smiled. 'I should have said protecting *his* kids, not *the* kids. In all our conversations he had talked about *the* kids, not *his* kids. If he'd recently found out that she had been lying to him for the past few years what makes him think that she hadn't lied earlier?'

'Good job, detective.' She smiled.

'If he discovered that the kids weren't his, you're suggesting this could send him over the top? And all of sudden want to get rid of her? Then to start planning the evidence and alibis so that we won't look that far.' He stopped, deep in thought.

Jean said 'it's just hypothetical.'

Cooper jumped up with new energy. That must be the missing piece. He already had formed an action plan. He knew he could search websites and hospitals to see if anyone had requested a DNA test and match this to the husband, motive proved...

Jean startled him. 'Sit down big boy!'

Cooper stopped halfway to the phone, then slowly turned and sat down.

'Now hear this before you run off being a detective' Jean added. 'Think about what you are doing, don't think like a detective, think like a father. If you find a clinic that has recently performed a couple of DNA tests for that address, and if you get access to the results, what are the consequences? Who suffers?'

Cooper sighed but listened.

'Do you think that man will love the kids less if they aren't his, or even if just one isn't? He has sacrificed so much to keep his family together that it really won't matter. And if the results show he is, or isn't, the father, what change will that make?'

Sometimes it's better not to know things. Sometimes life can be cruel, a well of despair, and when you get to the bottom there's only one way to go – up. Cooper knew she was right. She had a way of seeing further, the wider picture, than he had been trained to.

'You think I should just let it go?' he said.

'I never tell you what to do, I just point out the consequences, but for what it's worth I think that he has suffered enough. Do you think the children have suffered enough as well? People break up every day. Sometimes keeping a family together is not the answer, but I don't think people should be punished for trying at all costs.'

CHAPTER 35

THE BOTTOM OF THE WELL

I waited for about 10 minutes after they left, then sat on the settee and closed my eyes. I guessed it was over; no trial for anybody, no blame, no issue. Did she deserve better? At least Luke and Taylor would be spared.

Eventually I got out of my chair and walked upstairs. From the back of one of the cupboards I took out an old lined jacket and took it downstairs. With a pair of scissors I carefully unpicked some recent stitching and drew out the envelope that had been hidden there. Then I put the jacket down, took the envelope and its contents across the room and sat down near to the open fire. I pulled out the two slips of paper. Apart from the computer that had printed it and the people at the clinic, only Kate and I had seen the contents, I was sure, and only I knew that both of us had seen it. It was difficult to find out what had been going on last month but I knew something had been seriously amiss; she had gone into meltdown. At first I thought she was seeing someone else and although I had given up on the relationship I didn't want her still living with us whilst loving someone else.

Then, entirely by accident, I had come across her old jacket in one of the cupboards and realised that it was out of place there. I had bought it for her one Christmas and she had never worn it, but then all of a sudden it had appeared at the back of the cupboard. It didn't take me long to find that an envelope had been stitched inside the lining. Of course I read it and put it back.

When I first saw the contents, what I read really threw me. I was physically sick in the bathroom. Then I had to return it and clean up my mess before she came home, and that took some doing with my hands shaking. I avoided her all evening, pretended that I had a bad stomach, and went to bed early. When we had being seeing Kaz the therapist, she had told me to say whatever I wanted to say, not to keep it in, but this was big. I knew that if I confronted her with this information I would end up in jail for murder, but that night I knew I had to do something.

I spent another night without sleep carefully and deliberately considering each possible scenario to find a solution.

The letter was from a private clinic in Harley Street, London, with 'Private and Confidential' stamped on the front of the envelope. When I first read it I remembered the first line and the last line, but the main part of the letter was just a blur, noise to my eyes. It had begun something like: 'in respect to the two paternity tests that you sent us I am pleased to provide the results below'. Pleased? *Pleased?* Definition of 'pleased': 'feeling or showing pleasure and satisfaction, especially at an event or a situation'.

After all we had been through, I couldn't take finding out that not one but both my children were not mine. Yet it was now up to me to protect them.

I walked back downstairs and sat down in front of the open fire, then read the documents one more time, as some kind of justification for my actions. They were dated January 16th, the day before our last visit to the therapist, so she must have sent off for the results just before Christmas. All those promises had been just dust in the wind.

As I tore the papers into shreds and dropped them

into the burning fire, I said a silent prayer. I vowed to protect these children to the day I die, with all my strength. I would give them the life they deserved, and no one would ever know that I was not their father. If anyone found out I would kill.

Again.

There must be lights burning brighter somewhere
Got to be birds flying higher in a sky more blue
If I can dream of a better land
Where all my brothers walk hand in hand
Tell my why, oh why, oh why can't my dream come true
There must be peace and understanding sometime
Strong winds of promise that will blow away
All the doubt and fear
If I can dream of a warmer sun
Where hopes keep shining on everyone
Tell me why, oh why, oh why won't that sun appear
We're lost in a cloud, with too much rain
We're trapped in a world, that's troubled with pain
But as long as a man can dream
He can redeem his soul and fly
Deep in my heart there's a trembling question
Still I am sure the answer gonna come somehow
Out there in the dark there's a burning candle
And while I can walk, while I can talk
While I can stand, while I can walk
While I can dream, please let my dream... come true.

EPILOGUE

Hi, Joe here again. So what do you think? Does the end justify the means? Can I live with the secret, or should the boys know? Did I kill her or just help her to kill herself?

When you look back at things in your life the theory is that life evens itself up, the good times and the bad times, but what do I know? I'm just an old man who wants to look forward but can't see very far ahead.

Let me know what you think.